From the Chicken House

Can we ever imagine life for ordinary 'Joes' in the chaos and confusion of the First World War trenches? Well, here in this moving, heartbreaking and warm story Rebecca Stevens does just that – she takes a modern young girl back to meet a boy soldier and his dog. They learn a lot together – but more importantly they help each other come to terms with what's happening in both their worlds, when death becomes part of everyday life.

Sorry, I couldn't help crying. IT MUST NEVER HAPPEN AGAIN!

Barry Cunningham
Publisher

VALENTINE JOE

Rebecca Stevens

2 Palmer Street, Frome, Somerset BA11 1DS
www.doublecluck.com

Text © Rebecca Stevens 2014

First published in Great Britain in 2014
The Chicken House
2 Palmer Street
Frome, Somerset, BA11 1DS
United Kingdom
www.doublecluck.com

Cover and interior design by Helen Crawford-White
Cover photograph (boy) © CollaborationJS/Arcangel Images
Cover photograph (poppy) © iStock/April30
Cover photograph (dog) © Susan Schmitz/Shutterstock.com
Typeset by Dorchester Typesetting Group Ltd
Printed and bound in Great Britain by CPI Group (UK) Ltd, Croydon, CR0 4YY

The paper used in this Chicken House book is made from wood grown in sustainable forests.

3 5 7 9 10 8 6 4 2

British Library Cataloguing in Publication data available.

ISBN 978-1-909489-60-8
eISBN 978-1-909489-61-5

*In memory of my grandfather, Fred Thompson,
and the men and boys of all nations
who didn't make it home from the Great War.*

'In Flanders fields the poppies blow
Between the crosses, row on row,
That mark our place; and in the sky
The larks, still bravely singing, fly
Scarce heard amid the guns below.'

John McCrae 'In Flanders Fields', *Essex Farm 1915*

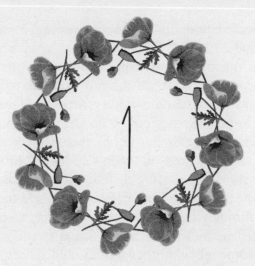

1

It was the day before Valentine's Day and Rose was on a train, speeding through the misty Kent countryside with her passport in her bag, her phone in her pocket and her grandad on the seat opposite, snoring gently. Rose hoped he wasn't going to dribble.

She stifled a yawn and looked around the compartment at the other passengers, trying to imagine who they were and what their lives were like. She often did this when she was sitting on a train or bus and had nothing else to do. It stopped her getting bored.

Or thinking about other stuff.

Her eyes rested on a smartly dressed woman across the aisle, working on her laptop. She lived on her own, Rose decided, in an amazing flat overlooking the river, but secretly longed to move to the country and breed guinea pigs. And the smug, pink-faced businessman opposite, who looked like he'd been over-inflated with a bicycle pump – he didn't know his teenage daughter had just got her tongue pierced and his son was keeping a snake in a shoebox under his bed. The young couple with backpacks and blond dreadlocks, whispering to each other further down the carriage, were on the run from the police. Rose was just trying to decide what crime they might have committed when the girl looked up and caught her eye.

Rose stared down at her book, cheeks hot with embarrassment. She seemed to spend a lot of time feeling awkward these days. She'd felt excited that morning though, when Grandad had picked her up and they'd gone swinging through the early-morning streets in a cab, heading for St Pancras International. She'd felt like someone different, someone who got on trains and set off to foreign countries all the time. Someone who found it easy to talk to boys, went to loads of parties and didn't spend so much time staring out of her bedroom window or making up weird stories about strangers on trains. Someone normal, in other words.

Someone happy.

Not that Rose was *un*happy. She didn't go round bursting into tears in Tesco or anything like that (although she did once feel like crying when a friendly bus driver called her 'sweetheart' and told her to have a good day). It was just that since it happened, since Dad died, Mum had been so wrapped up in her own sadness that you couldn't get near her. Rose felt the same in a way. It was like she and Mum were in two separate bubbles, floating away from each other in space. It had been nearly a year now, and Rose still felt a bit – *alone*.

She wasn't really alone, not literally. She *did* have Mum, of course she did, and Grandad. And her two best friends, Ella and Grace, had been extra nice to her.

But, but, but . . .

Rose's dad was thirty-eight when he died. He had sticky-up hair and a crooked grin. For months after, Rose had had the same dream. She'd be asleep in bed – in the dream – and there'd be a knock at the front door. And she'd wake up – still in the dream – and run down and open the door and there he was. Dad was there, looking just the same. And he'd grin and shrug and say: 'It was all a mistake! I'm here! Here I am!' And he'd hold out his arms and she'd feel the roughness of his jumper on her face and dissolve into the old familiar smell of soap and toast and bicycle oil.

And then she'd wake up, for real this time, and realise it was a dream. Dad had gone and she was alone in her room with the grey London morning seeping through the curtains and no one but her old teddy bear for company. She'd hear Mum getting breakfast downstairs and even the clatter of the plates would sound lonely. Then Rose would get up, get dressed, get on the bus to school. And at the end of the day, she'd come home and there'd still be no Dad, and Mum would still be silent and sad, and nothing would ever change, ever ever ever.

That was when she wanted to go back into the dream. And stay there for good.

Grandad made a little sound in his sleep and shivered. One of his hands was on the table between them: square-cut nails, brown spots on the back, veins standing out. Rose's heart clenched as she looked at it. Grandad was so *old*. He wouldn't be around for ever.

Rose couldn't bear to think what a world without Grandad would be like, so she reached out a hand to wake him. She wanted him to be there with her, to talk about normal stuff, make her laugh, start embarrassing conversations with strangers, anything. Then, as a funny little half-smile passed across his sleeping face, she changed her mind. She'd let him sleep. Her dad was his son, his boy. He missed him too. And perhaps, like Rose, he was dreaming about a knock on the door.

So Rose got out her phone instead and scrolled through the names. *Home, Ella, Grace, Grandad, Mummob, Dadmob* . . .

She clicked on *Dadmob*.

No one knew she still sent him texts. Not Mum, not Grace or Ella. Not even Grandad. It was her secret.

She'd sent the first one the day of the funeral. Everybody had come back to the house after the service for cups of tea and sandwiches, and Rose had sat by herself in the chair where Dad always sat to watch the football, a small knot of unhappiness, while the room, the guests, swirled anti-clockwise around her. Someone had dropped a salmon sandwich on the carpet near Dad's chair, which someone else had trodden on (the smell of tinned salmon still made Rose feel sick). She'd got out her phone to try and look busy, and scrolled through the numbers in her contacts. *Home, Ella, Grace, Grandad, Mummob, Dadmob* . . .

Dadmob . . .

Dadmob . . .

Dad . . .

She couldn't bring herself to delete it. That would make it real, the fact that he was gone. Final. So, sitting there, in his favourite chair, she'd sent him a text instead. Five words:

Hello dad it's me rose

Then a kiss, just one:

x

The thought of the words flying up through the air had made her feel a tiny bit better. So she'd been doing it ever since. She didn't write anything important or weird, just the usual stuff:

I'm on the bus and I'm bored x
History exam today argh x

Sometimes she just put:

x x x

Rose wondered what happened to all the texts she sent. She pictured them flying up, suspended against the blue of the sky for an instant before slithering down and ending up in a drift at the bottom like dead leaves. Then Dad would come along and stare at them for a second, before crouching down to sift through them and reassemble her messages:

I miss you
I'm sad
I don't want to be here if you're not

Sometimes she wondered how she'd feel if she got a reply. It'd probably be from someone who'd taken over the number:

Who r u? Stop txtng me freak!

'Fnuff!' Grandad made a loud snort and woke himself up. He looked around accusingly as if he didn't know where he was and glared at the woman working on her laptop before his eyes came to rest on Rose and his face softened. For a second he looked so much like Dad that Rose felt her eyes prickle.

'All right, Cabbage?'

Grandad was the only one who called her that now. Rose shook her head at him, pretending to be cross.

'You were snoring, Brian.'

When she was little Rose had heard her grandma calling Grandad by his first name and had copied her. This amused everyone so much she'd kept it up.

'When you get to my age snoring's one of the few pleasures you've got left,' he said, producing a plastic box from his bag. 'Have a biscuit.'

'No thanks, Grandad, you're all right.'

He opened the box and Rose got a whiff of custard creams. Their sweet, dusty, old-people smell didn't fit with the glossy new-car scent of the train.

'Please yourself. Look, we're about to go into the tunnel.'

Outside the windows the misty grey fields were now hidden by great blank walls going up on each side. Then there was a gentle *whoomp* and the pressure inside the compartment changed as the train entered the tunnel. The other passengers shifted in their seats and shared glances, as if something exciting was happening. Even the woman with the laptop, and the over-inflated businessman – who probably did the journey several times a week – looked up from their work to stare into the darkness outside the windows.

Rose could see her own face, ghostly in its cloud of dark hair, reflected in the darkness, as if another train were travelling alongside with another Rose on board. Was that train going to the same place, she wondered, or would it veer off somewhere else entirely when they left the tunnel? It was just like an ordinary train tunnel, actually. You'd never know you were going under the sea. *Dad would've enjoyed it though*, she thought. He'd have made up stories about mermaids being disturbed and swimming after the train, tails swishing angrily and hair streaming out behind them like seaweed. She texted:

In tunnel on way to belgium with grandad to look at war graves?!?! x

There was no signal in the tunnel, of course, but she pressed 'Send' anyway.

She was doing this for Grandad, this trip to Belgium. They were heading for a city called Ypres (you pronounced it 'Eepra', Mum had told her before they left) to visit his uncle's grave. Grandad couldn't fill the hole that Dad had left, but he tried his best and Rose loved him for that. So when he'd suggested the trip, Rose had said she'd go, even though it would mean she might miss Grace's Valentine's Day party. She didn't mind too much about that, actually.

'Have a look at this, Cabbage.' Grandad was rummaging in the old army surplus shoulder bag he always carried with him. His possessions soon covered the table: wallet, house keys (with keyring featuring photo of Rose aged seven looking embarrassed in primary school uniform), football whistle (Grandad coached a local boys' team), tube of stuff to rub on bad backs (smelling of old people), and then . . .

'What's that, Grandad?'

It was an old photograph mounted on yellowing cardboard which looked like it had once been in a frame. As Grandad pushed it across the table towards her, Rose caught a musty smell like old library books. It smelled of the past.

'It's my dad,' he said. 'Your great-grandad.'

Dad's grandad, thought Rose. Did they look alike? She looked at the young face in the photo, searching for similarities.

Grandad seemed to guess what she was thinking. Their eyes met for a second. Grandad was the first to look away.

7

'And that's his brother.' He pointed to the other young man. 'My uncle George.'

They were in uniform, the brothers, sitting on a bench in a photographer's studio with a potted palm behind them, gazing calmly out of the sepia-tinged past into Rose's eyes.

'It was taken just before they left,' Grandad continued.

'To the war?'

'Yeah, the Front. Flanders, in Belgium, where we're headed.'

Rose looked at the faces of the two young men in the photograph and wished she could tell them not to go.

'They look really young,' she said.

Grandad sighed. 'They were, Cabbage. Dad was nineteen, George a couple of years older. Boys.' He stared at the photo. 'Just boys.'

Rose fiddled with the silver chain round her neck. It had a tiny heart-shaped locket hanging from it, also silver. Mum and Dad had given it to her the Christmas before last. The locket opened up, but Rose hadn't yet found anything she wanted to put inside.

'Your dad was wounded, wasn't he, Grandad?'

Grandad didn't seem to hear. He was still looking at the photo, lost in thought.

'Grandad?'

'What? Oh, yes, yes. That's right, wounded. Bit of shrapnel in his bum, gave him gyp for years. But he was lucky, got sent home before the war was over. Whereas Uncle George—'

'He died, didn't he?' Rose had heard the story before.

Grandad nodded. 'My dad never got over it, not really. Felt bad about it all his life.'

'It wasn't his fault!'

Grandad sighed and gently touched the face of the young man in the photograph. 'Not the point, Cabbage.'

'But why should he feel bad? It doesn't make sense.'

'I know, love,' he said. 'I don't understand either. All I know is, Dad always wanted to go back to Belgium and find out where George was buried. Say goodbye, you know.'

Rose nodded. Goodbyes *were* important. She'd never had a chance to say goodbye to Dad. 'Why didn't he?'

'Life took over, I s'pose. He got married . . . then us lot came along.'

Grandad was the youngest of six boys. Rose had vague memories of two of them, Uncle Norman and Uncle Les. Big, laughing, jokey men who smelled of beer and cigarettes and the stuff they put on their hair and who let you walk around the room standing on their feet. Grandad was the little one of the family – an afterthought, he'd always said.

'So now we're doing it for him,' said Rose. 'Saying goodbye, I mean.'

'Yeah.'

The look on Grandad's face as he put the photograph back in his bag made Rose glad she'd agreed to come.

Whoomp . . .

The pressure inside the carriage changed again and daylight streamed through the windows as the train came out of the tunnel. Now they were passing through a flat pale landscape under a bleached wintry sky. Rose looked out of the window, and to her amazement saw a field containing a single ostrich.

'*Grandad!*'

Grandad's mouth fell open and his face took on an

expression of delighted astonishment. He looked like a little kid who'd just been given the most wonderful, unexpected, extraordinary Christmas present.

'An *ostrich*?' he said. 'In *Belgium*?'

'Could be an emu,' said Rose, trying to keep a straight face.

'An emu?!' shouted Grandad. Rose knew that would push his buttons. 'That's never an emu! I know an emu when I see one, my girl! And that – that thing out there – is an ostrich!'

The woman with the laptop and the over-inflated businessman were both looking at them. Rose was beginning to feel sorry she'd pointed it out.

'Oh, I've seen it all, now,' said Grandad, sitting back in his seat with a sigh. 'An ostrich in Belgium. I can die happy.'

He took another biscuit and Rose carried on looking out of the window. They were passing a farmhouse now. With its clean white walls and pitched red roof, it looked like an illustration in a children's book. Next to it was a barn, a field with a donkey in it, and a pond, almost completely round, with two cheerful-looking white ducks.

'Shell hole,' said Grandad, through a mouthful of biscuit.

Rose didn't understand. 'What?'

'That pond. Made by a shell in the war. That's why it's so round. Boom!' he added, unnecessarily, showering Rose with crumbs.

Rose looked back at the pretty round pond with its two happy ducks and imagined earth, trees, soldiers being thrown up into the air by the explosion, leaving the pond-shaped hole behind. She felt sick. How could something so pretty, so normal, so *nice* have come from something so horrible? It wasn't right.

Grandad was looking concerned. 'You OK, love?'

Rose forced a little smile. 'Yeah,' she said, even though she wasn't.

'Sure?'

'Sure.'

He put his head on one side, looking at her more closely. 'Surey-sure?'

'Surey-sure, Grandad.'

This was a game they'd played since she was little but Rose felt she was getting a bit old for it now.

'Surey-surey sure-sure?'

'Grandad!'

Out of the corner of her eye, Rose saw that the woman had stopped working on her laptop and was listening with a smile.

Grandad grimaced. 'Sorry, love. I just wouldn't want—'

'I'm fine, Grandad. Really.'

Grandad opened his mouth to speak again, but Rose got there first. 'And, no – I'm also sure I don't want a biscuit!'

He grinned. 'I'm glad you came with me, Cabbage. It wouldn't be the same on me own.'

'I'm doing it in history at school, you know – World War One.'

'History? Tuh!' Grandad made a dismissive sound with his false teeth. 'It's not proper history. Not if there's people you know in it.'

Rose thought that was silly. 'You didn't know your uncle George.'

'Not the point. History should be about strangers – kings, prime ministers, people no one cares about. This is too close!'

Grandad was having one of his rants. Getting up on his high hobby horse, Dad always used to say. Rose glanced over at the woman with the laptop but she looked engrossed in her work.

'World War One's not history!' Grandad went on. 'It's life!'

Rose wasn't sure. It didn't feel much like life to her. It felt like it had happened a very long time ago to people with funny haircuts and old-fashioned names like Albert and Walter and Sidney.

'If you ask me,' Grandad was saying, 'you should be doing more long-ago history. The Wars of the Roses' – he made them sound all silly and pompous – 'that sort of stuff. Proper history.'

Rose wasn't listening. They'd just passed another of those perfectly round ponds. She shivered. It was as if this neat, pretty landscape was hiding something horrible, like a bright new carpet covering a filthy old floor.

'Heads up!' Grandad was checking his watch. 'It's getting on for lunchtime. We'll be coming into Brussels soon.'

Rose pulled her eyes away from the window. 'What happens at Brussels, Grandad?'

'We have a sandwich!' he replied, triumphantly.

'And then?'

'We get on another train. To Wipers.'

'Wipers?'

'That's what the soldiers called it, the Tommies,' he said. 'Easier to say than Ypres, y'see. Unless you're French, obviously.'

Ypres. *Eepra.* That name again. It sounded like a little scream.

Fields were giving way to streets and houses now. As the train entered the city and began to slow down, the people in the carriage fell silent. The woman closed her laptop and stared into space, her fingers twiddling her wedding ring. The over-inflated businessman put his phone away and sighed. For a moment he looked so sad Rose thought he was going to cry. The backpackers had stopped whispering to each other and were looking out of the windows on opposite sides of the carriage, each lost in thoughts of their own. The only sounds were the rhythm of the wheels and the hum of the air conditioning.

'Angel passing over.'

It was what Grandad always said at these strange moments when everyone fell silent at the same time. Rose looked around at the faces of their fellow passengers, frozen in that one brief moment in time, and she thought, *Is it an angel? Or is it something else?*

As the train pulled into the station, the silence hung in the air like dust.

I eper.
  That's what it said on the station platform sign. Not Ypres. Ieper.

'Grandad?' Rose pointed to the sign as they got off the train. 'Are you sure this is the right stop?'

'Yup,' said Grandad. He landed his suitcase with a bump and slammed the train door. 'This is it all right.'

Rose followed him as he set off down the platform, dragging her case behind her. A few people had got off at the same time: a couple with a little boy who looked at Rose solemnly from under his fringe; a young woman with a briefcase; an elderly lady with an invisible cat yowling in a basket. They all hurried off to wherever they were going, leaving Rose and Grandad behind.

'Why doesn't it say Ypres?' said Rose. 'I can't even read that word.'

'It's the Flemish name,' said Grandad. 'Ieper. That's what they call it now. Ypres is the old name, the French

14

name.'

So this city's got three names, thought Rose. She repeated them to herself in her head – *Ieper, Ypres, Wipers* – and wondered which one it liked best. Then she felt a bit silly. Cities didn't have feelings, did they?

'This way!' Grandad had spotted the exit. 'Follow me!'

Outside the station was a car park where Rose saw the lady with the cat basket climbing on to a bus. It was grey and cold and flat, and the wind seemed to blow right through Rose's new parka, the one Mum had bought her for Christmas. It was very dark green with fur round the hood and she knew it had cost more than Mum could afford. Rose huddled down inside it, wishing she'd brought some gloves.

And then she saw the dog.

He was sitting outside the station as they came out, and was right in the middle of the path, blocking their way. It was almost as if he'd been waiting for them.

'Hello, you,' said Rose. She always spoke to dogs, whether she knew them or not.

The dog looked up at her and wagged his tail. He was quite a small dog, black and white and scruffy-looking, with serious-looking eyebrows and a hint of a beard. He looked friendly and tough at the same time.

'He can't understand you, Cabbage,' said Grandad. 'Belgian dog, see. Doesn't speak English.'

Rose held out her hand to the dog, with the fingers curled up into a fist like Dad had shown her. He gave it a polite sniff and then looked back at her face. There seemed to be a question in his bright brown eyes.

'How do you say hello in Flemish then, Grandad?'

'Don't ask me,' he said. 'It's a difficult language.'

Rose crouched down beside the dog and ruffled his head. The fur felt coarse under her fingers. She'd always wanted a dog. She and Dad used to talk about them a lot – which were their favourite breeds, stuff like that. They'd agreed that mongrels were the most interesting because they were all different. If you had a pedigree dog, a Labrador, say, it would look just the same as all the other Labradors. But you never knew what you'd get with a mongrel. They could be big, small, hairy, soft, black, white, brown, anything. This one was perfect.

'Don't you think we should try and speak a bit of Flemish while we're here, Grandad?' she said, scratching the dog's ears. 'Just to be polite?'

'Nah,' said Grandad. 'I reckon we can get by with speaking English in a funny voice.' Rose looked at him, not sure if he was joking. And then he said 'Hallooooo!' in a ridiculous accent, so she knew he was.

'That is never Flemish for hello,' she said.

'It is, actually,' said Grandad, pretending to be hurt. 'I've got a phrase book.' Rose continued to scratch the dog's ears, while Grandad rummaged in his bag. 'I bought it especially. In Waterstones,' he added in a prim voice. He produced the book, turned a couple of pages and then shouted, *'Alstublieft!'*

The word sounded exactly like a sneeze. The dog looked startled and gave Rose a look that seemed to say, *Is he with you?* She smiled and stroked his back. She could feel his ribs under the fur.

'Bless you,' she said to Grandad.

'It means "please",' he explained. 'Very important word. Useful when you want to ask for stuff. Biscuits, for example.'

'*Biscuits*?'

'Oh yes. Belgium's famous for 'em. Everybody knows that.'

'How d'you say that word again?'

Grandad checked his book and then repeated it, making it sound even more like a sneeze: '*Alstublieft!*'

'I'm never going to remember that.'

Grandad looked pleased, as if he'd won an argument. 'Told you it was a difficult language,' he said.

Rose sighed. Her knees were starting to hurt from crouching down by the dog. 'They speak French here too, don't they?' she said as she stood up. 'Maybe he's a bilingual dog. I could say *bonjour*.'

'You could,' said Grandad, putting on his most serious face. 'But you might look a bit daft. Talking French to a dog.' He grabbed the handle of his suitcase. 'Come on. Let's find our hotel.'

'Hang on, Grandad—' Rose looked down at the dog. 'Do you think he's a stray?'

Grandad paused. 'No collar,' he said. 'But he looks healthy enough.'

'He's a bit skinny. I could feel his bones when I was stroking him.'

'Tough-looking little chap, though, Cabbage. I reckon he can look after himself.'

'Maybe, but—'

'And we can hardly take him to the hotel with us, can we? I bet he belongs to someone. Probably lives round here.'

Rose wasn't sure. There was something about the dog that made her feel responsible for him. It wasn't just that she was afraid he was a stray. It was the way he looked at her, as if he was trying to tell her something. But before she could say anything, he got up and trotted off with his tail in the air, casting a quick look back over his shoulder as he went. So that was that.

Rose just stood there, watching him go, but Grandad struck a dramatic pose and called after him, waving.

'*Vaarwel! Vaarwel, mijn vriend!*'

Rose stared at him, open-mouthed.

'Flemish for goodbye, Cabbage.'

'I guessed that much – farewell. What did the second bit mean?'

'What, the bit that sounded like "my friend"?' He made a big show of looking in the book. 'Ah yes, here it is. It means "my friend".'

Rose gritted her teeth. Sometimes Grandad could be quite annoying.

He snapped the book shut and twinkled at her, thoroughly delighted with himself. 'I'm not just a pretty face, you know.'

Rose shook her head. He really was unbelievable.

'Right. What we need now is the map. Map map map . . .'

He rummaged in his bag again and pulled out a single crumpled sheet of A4 that he'd printed out before they left. After studying it for a bit, then turning it the right way up and studying it some more, he announced, 'This way!' and they set off across the car park and into the city.

Rose was nearly as tall as Grandad now, and he had a slight limp from having polio as a boy, but she still found it hard to keep up. He walked faster than anyone she knew.

'They rebuilt it after the war, you know, the city.' Grandad had done his research before they left, and was determined to share it. 'Every brick, every stone, was put back, exactly as it had been. There was nothing left in 1918, not a thing. It had all been blasted to smithereens. '

Rose looked along the street. It was neat and pretty, lined with houses built of light-coloured brick, quite unlike the warm red of the houses in Rose's street back home. But there was something strange about it. It was almost *too* neat, *too* pretty, like the pond they'd seen from the train. Even the people seemed too perfect: the woman riding past on an old-fashioned bicycle with a bunch of flowers in the basket; the rosy-faced children skipping hand in hand along the pavement . . . they looked too good to be true, like they were extras in a film or something, not real people at all.

It's like the city's a copy of itself, thought Rose. *A clone.*

She shivered. There was a sort of shimmer in the air and she imagined she could feel the pulse of something under her feet, like a heartbeat or the bass-line of a song heard from a long way off. It was as if the old city was lying asleep beneath the pavements, and, like Sleeping Beauty, was waiting for someone to come and wake her up.

'Look, Cabbage!'

'Wow!'

Mum had told Rose that Belgium was famous for its chocolate shops but she hadn't expected anything like this. The window they'd stopped outside was full of hearts: heart-shaped boxes of chocolates, chocolate hearts wrapped in red foil, shiny gold hearts hanging from pink ribbons . . .

Dad used to give Mum roses every Valentine's Day, one for each of the years they'd been together. She'd shake her head at him and say they couldn't afford it, but then she'd hug them to her chest and bury her nose in them even though they didn't smell (shop-bought roses never did, Dad said). Rose always got something too, something small, like a chocolate heart or a tiny cake in a box. It had started when she was little, so she wouldn't feel left out, but then it had become a tradition. This year would be the first Valentine's Day it didn't happen.

As Rose stepped away from the window and its display of memories, three things happened at once.

There was a shout from Grandad: 'Rose!'

Someone else shouted as well, words she didn't understand.

And she felt a thud in her back and a searing pain in her knee as she fell on to the road, breaking her fall with her hands.

Grandad rushed over, leaving his suitcase on the pavement.

'It's all right, Grandad, I'm fine . . .'

As Grandad took one arm and started to help her to her feet, Rose felt someone take her other arm and heard a voice, worried and apologetic:

'Het spijt me zo. Ik heb je niet gezien. Ik—'

Rose looked up to see a fair-haired boy of about her own age. He'd abandoned his bike on the pavement, where it lay next to their suitcases with one wheel spinning, forcing pedestrians to walk around it. He had a nice face with dark eyebrows, darker than his hair, and quiet grey eyes that met hers with a look of concern. As she struggled to her feet she felt uncomfortably aware of his hand under her elbow.

'It's fine,' she said. 'I'm fine. Thanks.'

Now go away, she thought. But he didn't. His face broke into a slow, sweet smile.

'You are English,' he said.

Rose still didn't want to look at him. It was her fault really, what had happened – she'd backed into his bike because she was thinking about Dad – but she wasn't about to admit that. She always felt a bit awkward with boys, even when she wasn't out in a weird little city in Belgium with her grandad. This was super-embarrassing.

'Are you sure, Cabbage?' Grandad looked worried too. 'You came a nasty cropper. Let me have a look at that knee.'

'No, really, it's fine. I'm OK, Grandad. Let's go.'

'I am very sorry,' the boy said. He spoke careful English with some sort of accent. 'I did not see you there.'

'It's OK.' Rose looked at the pavement. 'It was my fault.'

Go. Now. Just go!

'Your leg . . .? Is there something—?'

'NO!'

The word came out much louder than she'd intended.

'Sorry,' she said. 'I didn't mean – you know. Thanks for helping and everything, but—'

Grandad must have realised how much she was suffering, and decided to intervene. 'It's all right, young man. I think she'll live. You a local?'

Grandad was like Dad, any excuse to talk to a stranger. Mum used to say that when Dad went to the corner shop he'd come back with a pint of milk, a newspaper and seven new friends.

'Excuse me?' said the boy.

'Local!' Grandad raised his voice a notch. 'From around here? Belgian?'

The boy had gone to pick up his bike, but paused to

reply. 'Belgian? Me? Oh! No, no, I am here as a visitor. Like you.' He indicated their suitcases, then added, 'I am from Germany.'

'Germany?' Grandad sounded surprised. 'Well! I hope . . . you enjoy your stay.'

This was the boy's cue to leave, and he took it. 'Thank you,' he said, with a polite nod. 'I hope you do too.' And then, to Rose: 'And I hope your leg—'

'It's FINE!'

The boy nodded seriously. 'I am happy to hear that. Goodbye.'

'Bye!' The word burst out of Rose like an accusation. She felt bad. The boy must think she was really weird. 'I hope your bike's all right!' she called after him as he moved away, pushing his bike along the pavement. He looked back over his shoulder and gave a little wave before riding off down a side street. Rose and Grandad watched him go.

'German!' said Grandad. 'Well, well.'

'Well, well, what?' Rose asked. 'What do you *mean*, Grandad?'

Grandad shrugged. 'I don't know, Cabbage. I don't suppose they get too many German visitors, that's all. Come on.'

As Rose followed him down the street, the lights ahead shimmered and the ground seemed to shift under her feet. It was as if, beneath the modern pavements, the old city was stirring in her sleep.

3

The little shopping street opened out on to a huge cobbled space. Rose would've called it a square, except it wasn't square; it was a kind of misshapen rectangle, dominated by one massive building that bristled with so many towers and pointy bits that it looked like some kind of huge spiky creature.

'Cloth Hall.' Grandad was pleased to have another opportunity to show off his research.

'Cloth Hall?' repeated Rose.

'That's what it's called. Something to do with what it was originally used for. It's a museum now.'

'About the war?'

'About the war.'

They walked on past a low wall where a family of five sat in descending order of height licking ice creams. A stream of British schoolkids was tumbling off a coach. They were about Rose's age, she guessed, and were laughing and shouting and pushing each other, obviously excited their journey was over.

'Ow! Get off me!'

'Sir! Can we get ice creams, sir?'

'Where's the toilets, sir? Sir!'

A stressed-out teacher got off after them. 'Back here in twenty minutes, please!' he shouted. Nobody was listening. 'Twenty minutes, everybody! And that includes you, Josie!' A dark-haired girl wearing loads of make-up pulled a face before sauntering off after her friends.

It was funny, Rose thought, as she watched them scramble over to the public toilets and gather outside the windows of the chocolate shops, you could tell they were British even if you didn't hear them speak. It was something to do with their shouty daft humour and the way they teased their teacher. And their clothes, of course. Rose recognised a mint-green fake-fur bomber jacket from Topshop that Ella had wanted but couldn't afford, and a random pair of trainers from JD Sports.

'That's the one.' Grandad pointed to a building at the far end of the not-square square. 'The Old Town Hotel. That's where we're staying.'

The hotel was tall and narrow and perfectly symmetrical. It looked like a huge doll's house, waiting for a giant child to open it up and play with the furniture inside. Was it an exact replica of the building that had stood there before, Rose wondered. The thought made her feel dizzy and a bit sick, as if she was watching a 3D film without wearing the special glasses.

'Well, well, well,' Grandad was saying. 'Look who's here to meet us.'

'It can't be!'

But it was. There was no doubt about it. It was the same

dog, the one they'd met outside the station. He was sitting on the pavement in front of the hotel almost as if he was waiting for them again.

Grandad grinned. 'Chance for you to try out your French, Cabbage,' he said. 'See if he understands you. Go on, no one's listening!'

Rose was so glad to see the dog again that she couldn't speak. She ran over to him, leaving her suitcase with Grandad. The dog got up, wagging his tail so hard his whole body seemed to wag too. When Rose crouched down to stroke him, he rolled over on to his back, waggling his legs.

'Someone's pleased to see you.' Grandad arrived, dragging both suitcases behind him.

'I wonder what he's doing here? Do you think he followed us?'

'If he followed us,' said Grandad, 'he'd hardly have got here first, would he?'

'He must be a stray.' Rose scratched the dog's chest. 'He wouldn't have wandered this far if he lived near the station.'

Grandad looked down at the dog and sighed. 'You may be right,' he said.

'We could ask in the hotel.'

'We could indeed. Let's do that. And no,' he added, in answer to the question in Rose's eyes, 'you can't bring him in with us. Come on.'

So they left the dog outside watching them as they went inside.

The Old Town Hotel wasn't like the bed and breakfast that Rose had stayed in once with her mum and dad during a trip to the Lake District (they were meant to be camping, but it had been raining so much when they arrived that Mum said they'd treat themselves). It was a proper hotel, with fresh flowers and a rack of tourist maps and brochures. There was a polished wood floor and sepia prints of the ruined city on the walls. The whole place smelled deliciously of food and flowers and furniture polish and opposite the front door there was a grandfather clock whose tick broke up the silence.

'Look at these, Cabbage.' Grandad was examining three rusty metal objects like giant stretched-out bullets that were displayed on the reception desk. They were arranged on a sort of lacy table mat as if they were fancy cakes in the window of a teashop. Next to them was a laminated sign, written in English. It read: *'We found these shell cases when we were renovating the cellar. They had been there for nearly one hundred years.'*

Shell cases? From the war? Rose reached out a finger and touched one of them, then quickly withdrew it, feeling stupidly scared it might explode. Tiny bits of rust had stuck to her finger, which she wiped off on her parka.

'You're not going to set them off, Cabbage,' said Grandad. 'Not now.'

But Rose shuddered. She understood what Grandad meant now, about the history of this place being too close. These things belonged in a museum, safe behind glass, not displayed on a lacy mat in a hotel foyer.

'It feels like it's everywhere,' she said. 'The war. What must it be like to live here?'

'Oh, you'd get used to it,' said Grandad. 'People do. You can't spend all your time living in the past, can you?'

Can't you? Rose wanted to say. Sometimes she felt that living in the past was exactly what she wanted to do.

Because Dad was there. Since he died she'd felt like she was sleepwalking through her life. Dad's absence, his not-thereness, was with her all the time – not a second went by that she wasn't aware of it. Every tick of that grandfather clock, every beat of her own heart reminded her: *he's gone, he's gone, he's gone . . .*

Grandad patted her arm. He could tell when she was thinking about Dad. 'Life goes on, lovely,' he said. 'People get up, clean their teeth, make friends, have fun. They've got to if they're going to survive. *We've* got to.'

'I'm so sorry. Have you been waiting long?'

A woman had appeared from a door behind the counter. She was about Grandad's age with soft grey hair pulled back in a bun and a face that lit up when she smiled. Her accent was only very slight when she spoke English, but this didn't stop Grandad addressing her in the special voice he kept for foreigners.

'I have two rooms booked!' he shouted. 'Singles! One for myself! And one for my granddaughter!'

Rose looked at her feet. A small smile played around the woman's mouth as she checked the computer.

'Ah yes,' she said. 'It's Mr Thompson, isn't it? And Rose.'

Rose relaxed. The woman seemed so normal, so *nice*. She was silly to be afraid of this place.

'Just for the one night, yes?' the woman continued, reaching for their room keys. 'Have you come to visit the battlefields? Look for the grave of a relative?'

'My uncle,' said Grandad, forgetting to use his foreigners' voice. 'George. My dad always wanted to come – to say goodbye, you know. But he never made it. So we've come instead.'

27

The woman nodded. 'It's important, I think,' she said. 'To pay your respects to the past.' A faraway look came into her eyes. 'Here in Ieper we live with the past. The present is just a thin covering. Scratch it and the past reappears.'

For a second, no one spoke.

Angel passing over, thought Rose.

It was Grandad who broke the silence. 'You speak very good English!' he said. 'If I may say so. Very good indeed.'

'Most of our guests are from the English-speaking world,' the woman replied, with a smile. 'British, like you. Canadian. Australian. They all come to visit their people.'

'Their people?'

'The ones that never went home.'

In her mind's eye, Rose saw them, all those young men. She saw their sepia-coloured faces, their sad eyes, and felt their cold hands reaching out to touch her.

The woman pushed the keys across the counter. 'Breakfast is served in the restaurant between seven and nine-thirty. I hope you enjoy your stay.'

Rose nudged Grandad, who seemed to have gone into a bit of a trance. Perhaps he was thinking about George, the uncle that never went home.

He shook himself. 'Sorry, love. Ghost walked over my grave.'

The Belgian woman looked puzzled. 'Ghost . . .?'

'What? Oh, sorry, it's just an expression.' He took the keys. 'Thank you. Mrs, er—?'

'Muriel,' she said. 'Your room is number six at the top of the stairs, Mr Thompson—'

'Brian,' Grandad corrected her.

'Brian.' She smiled and turned to Rose. 'And I've given

you the room at the very top of the building because your legs are younger than those of your grandfather. I think you'll like it.'

As Grandad turned to go, Rose put a hand on his arm. 'What about . . .?' she hissed, jerking her head towards the front door.

'Oh yes,' he said and turned back to the hotel owner. 'Excuse me, Mrs – um – *Muriel*?'

Muriel looked up from her computer screen. 'Yes?'

'We saw a little dog outside. Don't know if you've spotted him around the place? Rose here took a fancy to him and we were wondering if he's a stray.'

Muriel looked puzzled. 'Stray?' She'd obviously not heard the word before.

'Lost,' explained Grandad. 'No owner. Homeless. Sad—'

Rose hoped he'd stop before he started on an impression of a stray dog. It was the sort of thing he'd do. Luckily Muriel interrupted.

'Ah!' she said. 'I understand. But no, I don't think so. I have not seen any lost dogs around here. What does he look like?'

Grandad shrugged. 'Smallish,' he said. 'Black and white . . .'

'Really really cute with big eyebrows and a beardy bit on his chin,' Rose broke in. 'He's the kind of dog that looks like he's grinning at you.'

Muriel smiled. 'I can see he made quite an impression.'

'He did, he's lovely!' said Rose. 'I'll check he's still there.'

She hurried to the door. Outside in the not-square square the schoolkids were drifting back towards their coach. But there was no sign of the dog. Rose was surprised at how disappointed she felt.

'Never mind, Cabbage.' Grandad had joined her at the door. 'He's probably gone home for his dinner.'

Rose bit her lip and nodded. She felt stupidly close to tears.

'We'll keep an eye out for him, though,' he patted her arm. 'Just in case.'

Muriel was right – Rose did like her room. It was a bit of a struggle getting up all the stairs with her suitcase (there was no lift) but it was worth it. It was the only one on the third floor, and it had sloping ceilings, a picture of some blurry poppies on the wall and a view across the square. Outside, the teacher was counting his students as they scrambled back on to their coach, and some elderly tourists wearing rainproof jackets in various shades of beige were looking doubtfully at a restaurant menu.

She texted Dad:

This city is weird old but not old will send photo x

She held up her phone to the window and took the photo. The teacher followed the last of the schoolkids on to the coach and slammed the door. One of the elderly tourists put up an umbrella.

Rose checked the image on her phone.

And then she checked it again.

Something wasn't right.

The square was there, looking just as not-square as usual, with its shops and restaurants. But where was the coach? The schoolkids? The elderly tourists?

Rose looked out of the window. Maybe the angle was a bit funny, and the coach had driven away faster than she thought. But no, the coach was just leaving the square now.

And she could see the tourists heading off to look at another restaurant.

But they weren't in the photo.

She looked at it again. You could make out a few people. But they weren't the ones she could see from the window. They definitely weren't. There was a man on a bicycle. A woman in a longish skirt, holding a child's hand. An old lady with a scarf over her head, carrying a basket of vegetables. But hang on, wasn't that . . .?

It looked like him.

It was.

The dog was there, in the photo, sitting outside the hotel, looking up at her window. Looking *at her.*

She stared at her phone. And while she was trying to make sense of what had happened, she heard a single bark. It was a quiet bark, polite almost, as if to attract her attention.

Rose looked up from her phone and out of the window. And there he was, sitting on the pavement, looking up at the hotel, just as he was in the photo. But if the dog was in the photo then why weren't the schoolkids? Or the tourists?

What was going on?

4

By the time Rose got out into the square, the dog had gone. Grandad was there, though, talking to Muriel and struggling to control an unfolded tourist map from the hotel which was threatening to blow away. Rose watched them, their grey heads close together over the map, until Grandad looked up and saw her. He had a red rose in his buttonhole.

'What's with the rose, Grandad?'

'What? Oh, this.' He looked down at it. 'Bought it from the flower shop over there. It's for Uncle George. Not that appropriate for a soldier boy, I know, but roses was all they had, it being Valentine's tomorrow. And the price!'

'Did Uncle George like roses?'

'I dunno. Can't turn up empty-handed, though, can we? Not after all these years. Muriel reckons we can walk.'

'Walk?'

'To the cemetery.'

'Your grandfather tells me his uncle is buried at Essex

Farm,' said Muriel. 'It's not too far away.'

'Essex Farm?' said Rose. 'That doesn't sound very Belgian.'

'They have kept the English names of many of the important sites,' Muriel explained. 'The ones given to them by the British soldiers: Tyne Cot, Lone Tree . . .'

'Hellfire Corner,' added Grandad, with relish.

'The cemetery's not far,' said Muriel. 'Just out of the city. You can walk along the canal.'

'You up for that, Cabbage? It looks like the rain'll hold off.'

Rose shrugged. The square looked quite ordinary now in the cold February light. 'I'm up for it if you are, Grandad.'

'Good girl. Now? This way!'

'I'll catch up with you in a sec, Grandad,' said Rose as he strode off. 'I just want to check something.'

She took her phone out of her bag and clicked on 'Photos'.

It had gone.

The photo. Had gone.

For a moment the ground seemed to sag beneath Rose's feet.

It doesn't mean anything, she told herself. *I must have deleted it by accident*. It was easily done, happened all the time. And there was nothing that strange about it anyway, it was just the angle she'd taken it from. She'd imagined it all. She was like that, always had been, Mum said – saw things that weren't there, heard whispers in the dark, footsteps on night-time pavements . . .

Once, when she was very little, she'd woken in the night to see a fairy standing on the end of her bed. It was quite a large fairy, about three feet tall, and had no wings, but Rose had known at once what it was. She hadn't been frightened, just thought, *Oh, a fairy*, and went back to sleep, as if waking up to find a fairy standing on the end of your bed was the most ordinary thing in the world. Mum and Dad had laughed when she told them about it in the morning, and then exchanged a private look which Rose wasn't meant to see. Grandad was interested, though, and told her about holidays in Ireland when he was a boy and his nan took him out hunting for leprechauns under the fuchsia hedges.

But she'd grown out of all that now. There was nothing strange about Ypres – nothing at all. It was just an ordinary little place where something terrible had happened a long time ago.

It didn't take long to reach the edge of the city. There was a canal that ended abruptly in a sort of dock area with a couple of barges, a warehouse and a block of flats, bleak against the rain-scratched sky. It was starting to drizzle.

'Was this a good idea, Grandad?' said Rose. 'We haven't got an umbrella.'

'Bit of rain won't hurt us,' he replied. 'We've got macs!'

'I know, but—'

'And if we're hungry, I've got plenty of biscuits. Come on, it's not far.'

They set off along the path at the side of the canal. It was wider than canals Rose had seen back home and in pictures of Amsterdam and Venice. The water was dark and slimy-looking. It seemed thicker than water, like treacle or oil, and slithered along past them, flexing like the muscle of some huge animal. It made Rose feel queasy and frightened, as if she might be seized by an uncontrollable desire to throw herself into its greasy depths.

She didn't, though. She just walked along beside her grandad, wondering what she was doing there. Back home Grace would be preparing for her party. Grandad had said they'd probably be back in time if Rose wanted to go, but she didn't want to, not really. She didn't like parties that much any more.

She used to love them, looked forward to them for days. There'd be long sessions with Grace and Ella round each other's houses, trying on outfits, doing each other's make-up (Mum didn't approve), discussing who'd be there and laughing helplessly for hours and hours about nothing in particular. There was one boy from school she'd liked, Lewis. He was tall and funny and handsome and good at football. Nearly all the girls liked him, but for some unknown reason Rose always got the feeling he liked her best. One time, in year eight, this girl in her class had a party and invited everyone, so Rose had known that Lewis would be there. She'd spent ages planning what to wear, longer than usual, even. Grace had lent her her new top and Ella had spent ages with the hair straighteners, ironing the kinks out of Rose's hair.

And then, when they got to the party, Lewis had spent all night talking to his friends and hadn't looked at Rose once. She'd felt so disappointed she thought the world would end.

It seemed silly now, to be so upset about something so little. But she was only just thirteen when it happened. A lot had changed since then. Lewis was going out with Daisy McCallister, the prettiest, most confident girl in the year. And Rose's dad had died.

She walked on, matching her pace to Grandad's. They passed an old man fishing from underneath a green nylon tent. Grandad greeted him with a nod and the old man raised a hand in reply. Rose wondered what sort of creatures might live in the dark, greasy waters of the canal, and imagined great eyeless eel-like things like giant leeches, with grey muscular bodies and circular mouths lined with jaggy teeth. She hoped no one would ever expect her to eat them.

The path was pretty, though, with overhanging trees and a few cheerful yellow flowers like buttercups among the long grass, brave little faces turned up to the pale February sky.

'Celandines,' said Grandad. 'My favourite.'

He knew about flowers. His dad, Arthur, had been a gardener's boy before he left to join the army. Maybe he and Uncle George had looked at the celandines when they were here and he'd told George what they were called.

'Terrible weed, of course,' Grandad was saying. 'Devil to get rid of once you've got them in your garden. But I've always liked them. Cheery little blighters, come out before anything else at the end of winter when there's no other flowers about.'

Rose liked them too, with their dark-green heart-shaped leaves. She picked a little bunch. Like Mum's Valentine roses, they didn't smell of anything, but they made her feel better. She hoped they'd made George and Arthur feel better too.

'The canal was the front line at one time,' Grandad was saying. 'We were on this side—'

'We'? Rose thought. *How come it was 'we' all of a sudden?* She didn't feel like she was on one side or the other. Wasn't it equally awful for everybody?

'—dug into the banks of the canal. And the Germans were over there.'

Beyond the water was a flat industrial area dominated by several giant wind turbines, their huge white arms turning lazily against the sky.

'So it was just the canal that divided them?' said Rose.

'No, there would've been some space between the two armies. No-man's-land, they called it. Because it didn't belong to either side. It would've been that area across the canal, I suppose.' He shook his head. 'Wonder what the Tommies'd think if they could see it now,' he went on. 'Blooming great what-d'you-call-'em, windmill things. Great arms waving around.'

Rose liked the turbines. They were like giant versions of those brightly coloured plastic windmills at the seaside. She remembered Dad buying her one in Brighton when she was little, and him and Mum laughing as she ran up and down the promenade to make it whizz round.

'Heads up,' said Grandad. He'd stopped and was looking through the hedge on their left. 'This must be it.'

A stone monument pointed up at the sky in a field where a cow peered at them with gentle eyes and a line of drool hanging from her mouth. They followed a path leading up from the canal and then they were at the gate: Essex Farm Cemetery.

Rose didn't know what she'd expected. Something bleak, grand, mournful. Vast. Graves stretching away into infinity, unimaginable numbers of men with names and no faces. Some of them without even names. Unknown soldiers.

But this wasn't like that at all. It was – *cosy*. Quite small, like a room almost, with trees on three sides, branches moving gently. The identical gravestones were lined up, shoulder to shoulder, like tiny upright beds. And there was no sound. No birds, no cars. Nothing except the gentle *whoomp whoomp* of the turbines on the other side of the canal. There was no one else there. Just Rose and Grandad and the men lying beneath the turf.

'They keep the grass nice, don't they?' Grandad's voice sounded loud in spite of the wind.

The grass *was* nice, bright green and velvety, as if it had just been vacuumed.

'Quite right, too,' he went on. 'Respect. Got to keep faith with the dead.'

Rose looked at the neat rows of identical gravestones and wondered if the soldiers lying there cared about the grass.

'Look at this, Cabbage.' Grandad had moved towards a row of cave-like concrete rooms cut into the bank near the cemetery entrance.

'What is it?'

Grandad was looking at his guide book. 'Advanced dressing station. First stop for the wounded when they were brought off the battlefield.'

'This was where the doctors treated them?' Rose couldn't believe it. 'In these tiny little caves?' None of the rooms was much bigger than the bathroom at home, and they stank of damp and decay.

'Yup. They patched them up here and then sent them on to a proper hospital, further away from the front line. Or home, if they were lucky.'

'What if they weren't lucky? Grandad?' Rose knew he didn't want to say. 'That's why the cemetery's here, isn't it?'

Grandad nodded. 'Yes, love. For the ones that didn't make it.' He harrumphed and changed the subject, making a big fuss of rummaging in his bag. 'Right, Uncle George, Private Thompson. I've got a reference number for him somewhere.'

'A reference number?'

'War Graves Commission. You get it off the internet. Surprisingly easy actually. Ah, here we go.'

Grandad produced a scrap of paper from his bag and made his way towards the cemetery, his limp more pronounced after their walk. He'd told Rose stories about being in hospital with polio when he was a boy after the war. Not this war, of course – the next one. How many wars did there have to be, before they stopped for good?

Rose lingered at the entrance, watching Grandad step carefully between the graves, looking at the numbers on the ends of the rows. Something was stopping her going into the cemetery. It felt sort of scary, like taking that first step into the classroom on your first day of school. Rose had clung to Dad's legs, hiding her face in the knees of his jeans until he'd peeled her off and given her a kiss and a gentle push into the hands of the teaching assistant. He'd said she'd be all right, and she was, she really was. But everything was different from that moment. Her world had changed from being just Dad, Mum, Grandad . . . kitchen, bedroom, park, corner shop. It had expanded to include school, teachers, dinner ladies, other children and an infinite number of new smells, sights, feelings, experiences. It wasn't a bad thing, it really wasn't. But it was big.

And this felt the same, as if she was teetering on the edge of something momentous. There was something here, in this place, buried deeper than the poor dead soldiers beneath the grass. Something that was in the past. But it was also here now, waiting.

Waiting for her.

Rose took a deep breath and took the step, the single step, into the cemetery. Nothing happened, of course. The world didn't explode or change colour. But something was different. It was like being in a house whose owner had just left, or Dad's studio in the attic back home. Everything was still there – his paints, his canvases, his old jumper on the back of a chair. Even though he was gone, the room was still full of his presence.

It was like that in the cemetery. Rose could almost feel the dead soldiers breathing under the grass.

It's a peaceful place to spend eternity, she thought, and took a few more steps, being careful not to stand on the graves. Across the cemetery she could see Grandad taking the rose from his buttonhole and laying it on the ground. He'd found Uncle George.

Rose tiptoed along the rows, reading the names on the headstones: Frederick, Henry, Alfred, Herbert. They sounded like old men with their old-fashioned names, but they weren't old, thought Rose, and they never would be. Then, surprisingly, a German name: Benedikt. His gravestone was different from the others, a bit rougher, more worn-looking. Poor Benedikt. Rose wondered how he'd ended up here, buried beside the men he'd been fighting.

And now, a stone with a Star of David in place of the usual cross:

A .G. Cohen
West Yorkshire Regiment
19th December 1915 Age 22
Rose thought of Mrs Cohen back in Yorkshire, crying in

her kitchen like her own mum had cried in their kitchen when Dad died. Was history full of mums crying in kitchens?

She walked on.

A grave in the middle of one of the rows caught her eye. It had more tributes than the others (most had none at all) – loads of the little papery crosses you could get everywhere in the city, a couple of bunches of shop-bought flowers, still in their cellophane, a small teddy bear wearing a poppy. That was weird. Why would anybody put a teddy on a soldier's grave?

Rose made her way towards it, and read:

V.J. Strudwick
The Rifle Brigade
14th January 1916 Age 15

Rose's heart clenched.

Fifteen?

Fifteen? That was only one year older than she was. How could that have happened? How could it be *right*?

"'Valentine Joe Strudwick . . .'" She hadn't heard Grandad approach. His voice sounded loud and reassuringly normal as he read from his guide book: "'. . . was one of the youngest soldiers known to have been killed in action in the Great War—'"

'Valentine?' Rose interrupted. So that was what the V was for. She looked at the headstone again. Beneath his name and age and the cross was another inscription:

Not Gone From Memory Or From Love

Who chose that? His mum?

'Name to give a boy, eh?' Grandad was saying. 'Born on Valentine's Day, you see. I blame the mother. No dad would give a boy a name like that.'

Of course, thought Rose. His mum chose them both: his name and the inscription on his gravestone. His poor mum. She thought again of her own mum and felt a pang. Maybe they should have persuaded her to come with them. Rose didn't like to think of her all alone. Especially not on Valentine's Day.

'Bet he called himself Joe,' Grandad was saying. 'Valentine! Tuh!' He made the dismissive sound with his false teeth that he always made when he disapproved of something.

Yes, thought Rose. *He would've called himself Joe.*

He could have been a boy at her school – slouching along the corridors at school, bag dangling off one shoulder, whacking a friend round the head and running off, laughing at nothing, kicking a football. Not fighting – *being killed* – in some grown-ups' war.

Grandad continued to read: '"Although the official age for active service was nineteen, many younger boys lied about their age in order to join up, probably inspired by propaganda campaigns at the time and the belief that war would be an adventure . . ."'

'But they must've known.' Rose felt angry. 'The army people, whoever was in charge. How could they not? There's no way a fifteen-year-old can pass for nineteen.'

Grandad read on. '"It's thought recruiting officers often turned a blind eye to underage recruits due to the urgent need for men to replace those that had been injured or killed at the Front . . ."'

'Oh, Grandad . . .'

Rose felt so furious at the people in the past who had let this happen that she was afraid she might start shouting and screaming and stomping round the cemetery. Either that or burst into tears.

Grandad put the book away and held out his hand. Rose took it and they stood there in silence, their heads bowed. She swallowed hard, determined not to cry.

'So you found Uncle George?' she said. Her voice sounded unnaturally high and cracky.

Grandad gave himself a little shake. He wasn't going to cry either. 'Yeah. Yeah, I did. I said, "Hello, George, mate. You don't know me, but I know all about you and I've come to say goodbye. And thanks." And I left the rose for him. I think he appreciated it.'

Rose smiled. The cemetery seemed to come back into focus and she was conscious of the gentle spikes of drizzle on her face and the *whoomp whoomp* of the turbines across the canal.

'Come on, Cabbage. Let's get you back to the hotel. It'll be getting dark soon.'

He patted her arm and moved off towards the gate. Rose lingered for a moment at the grave.

'It's your day tomorrow,' she whispered. 'Valentine Joe.' She put the yellow flowers with their heart-shaped leaves down next to the teddy bear.

'Happy birthday,' she said.

5

It was getting dark by the time they got back to the city, and the warm yellow lights from the bars and restaurants looked blurry in the twilight, as if they were shining through gauze. Rose was glad to be back. Her feet hurt from the long walk and her hair had gone all frizzy.

She left Grandad downstairs in the hotel, telling Muriel about their outing, while she went up to her room. They'd arranged to meet up later for the Last Post ceremony at the Menin Gate. Rose wasn't quite sure what it was, but Grandad wanted to go and that was enough for her.

She opened the door of her room, flumped down on the bed and was starting to take her boots off when something stopped her. The room was bright and cosy with its clean white walls and neat single bed. Everything looked completely normal, just as she'd left it: her suitcase open on the floor, phone charger plugged in by the bed. But there was something else. Rose sat quite still, listening with every part of her body.

Someone was singing.

It was a girl's voice, singing a high, wordless little song, as if she was pottering around tidying up. It was what Mum used to do in the kitchen while she was clearing away the breakfast things on a Sunday.

Rose got up and opened the door to the tiny shower room that adjoined the bedroom, fitted in neatly under the eaves of the building. There was no one there, of course, she hadn't expected there to be. But the voice was there, as clear as if its owner was in the room with her. She checked outside on the landing. Nothing.

And then it stopped.

It must've been someone next door, Rose told herself, then remembered there wasn't a room next door. Downstairs, then. Or outside – sound carried in a strange way in this kind of weather. It was nothing, just one of those funny things.

Rose sat down on the bed again and got out her phone to text Dad. But for the first time she didn't know what to say. Since she and Grandad had arrived in Ypres she'd felt different. There *was* something strange about the place, but she couldn't explain what. Not in a text, anyway. And she couldn't tell Dad about seeing Valentine Joe's grave, because she didn't understand her own feelings about that. It was all too strange, too big, too *weird*. So she plugged her phone into the charger and went to have a shower.

Maybe she'd text him later.

'It's not a gate though, is it, Grandad? It's an arch. A really big arch.'

It was nearly eight o'clock and Rose and Grandad were waiting with a lot of other people at the Menin Gate for the start of the ceremony of the Last Post. Grandad had put on a proper jacket and tie for the occasion.

'It would've been a gate at one time,' he said. 'Or at least a portal. A way through the city walls.'

'And the soldiers would've gone this way? To the Front?'

'Yup. And these' – Grandad indicated the thousands of names inscribed on the walls of the archway – 'are the names of those that didn't come back. Some of them, anyway.'

'Were they killed then, sir? All these people?'

It was the group of British schoolkids Rose had seen earlier. She recognised the mint-green fake-fur bomber jacket and the dark-haired girl with loads of make-up. There was also a Sikh boy she hadn't noticed before, who was using his phone to take photos of a list of Sikh soldiers on the wall next to him.

Rose wondered how those Indian soldiers must have felt, leaving their hot, brightly coloured continent and coming halfway across the world to this cold grey country to take part in someone else's war.

'All these names are the missing,' Grandad was saying. 'Men whose bodies were never found. Men who have no graves.'

The teacher was explaining the same thing to his students.

'No way, sir! There's so many!'

It was true. There were so very many. Every inch of the walls was covered, every inch, with name after name after name. There were too many to take in. Too many to be real people. Until you started to read the individual names – then they became real: *Private Campbell H, Corporal Day*

W, Sepoy Jagat Singh . . . Rose could see them in her mind's eye: young men with crooked smiles and sticky-up hair and families back home, boys like the boys she went to school with, who played football and liked a laugh and had love letters and photos in the pockets of their uniforms. Each one of them someone's boyfriend, someone's brother, someone's son. Someone's dad.

There was a movement and a rustle of expectation in the crowd. Everyone turned to the road, where four elderly gentlemen in blue blazers were standing in a line, gripping bugles in their right hands.

The crowd grew silent. There was a single giggle from the dark-haired girl but that was quickly shushed by her friend. The men raised their bugles to their lips and the sorrowful wail of the Last Post curled out into the night like smoke. It was slightly out of tune, but when Rose tried to swallow the lump she felt in her throat she found it wouldn't go away.

There was a minute's silence when the last notes of the bugles died away, filled only with a few coughs and awkward shuffles, then another elderly gentleman in a blue blazer stepped forward, moustache bristling with importance. His voice rang out, strong and confident under the silent white arch:

They shall grow not old, as we that are left grow old:
Age shall not weary them, nor the years condemn.
At the going down of the sun and in the morning
We will remember them.

A small procession of schoolchildren stepped forward to lay wreaths of poppies. And that was it.

The crowd gave a sort of collective sigh and people began to wander away. As Grandad and Rose joined the drift back to the city centre, Rose spotted the German boy who'd knocked her over with his bike. He was standing at the side of the road with a couple of other boys – one about his own age, the other a bit younger. As the boy raised his hand to Rose, his friend (or brother? Rose wondered) leant over and said something in his ear. Rose hid behind her hair and looked away.

'Pizza?' said Grandad.

'Pizza,' she agreed.

The night was clear by the time they left the restaurant. They'd sat at the next table to an Australian couple who said they'd come all the way from Adelaide to find the grave of a relative. Grandad told them about going to Essex Farm Cemetery to say goodbye to Uncle George and how they discovered Valentine Joe's grave. As she listened to the three older people exchanging stories and jokes, Rose thought Grandad seemed happier than she'd seen him since Dad had died. The trip was doing him good. That was what Mum would say anyway. But what was it doing for Rose? She wasn't sure.

It wasn't far back to the hotel. They said goodnight to Grandad's new friends and wandered down the short street towards the square, past the souvenir shops selling books and postcards and pieces of shrapnel. There were only a few stragglers in the square now, a couple holding hands and a man walking a dog. The bars and restaurants looked warm and inviting, the golden light from their windows spilling on to the wet cobbles.

Muriel was outside when they arrived at the hotel, talking to a waiter who'd come out for a cigarette. Her face lit up when she saw them. She'd been working in the restaurant, she explained, and wanted a breath of air before they closed up.

'I love the square at night,' she said in her careful English. 'It feels like the most beautiful place on earth. Come inside and have a last coffee or a drink.'

'What d'you reckon, Cabbage?' said Grandad. 'It's been a long day. D'you fancy a drink or do you want to head up to bed?'

Rose didn't feel tired, but she didn't want a drink either. Like the old city, stirring beneath the cobbles, she felt restless. Maybe it was because of what had happened today. She couldn't seem to get Valentine Joe out of her mind.

'I think I'll just walk around for a bit, actually,' she said. 'I'm not that tired.'

'You sure?'

Rose nodded.

'You'll be OK?'

'I'm fourteen, Grandad.'

'Ieper is a safe place, Brian,' added Muriel. 'Very quiet, very small . . .'

'Unlike London,' Rose reminded him. 'And I've got my phone.'

Grandad gave her a long look. 'Sure?' he said.

'I'm sure,' Rose replied, willing him not to do the 'surey-sure' thing in front of Muriel.

Grandad grinned and patted her shoulder. Sometimes he seemed to be able to read her mind. 'Put your head in the restaurant when you're back then, Cabbage.'

'I will.'

'Ten minutes?'

'Twenty!'

'Fifteen.'

She shook her head at him and rolled her eyes. He was such a fusspot sometimes.

'I promised your mum I'd look after you, Cabbage. So I need you back in one piece. OK?'

'OK, Brian.'

As Rose walked off into the darkness she looked back to see Grandad and Muriel watching her, standing together in the pool of light outside the restaurant. They raised their hands in reply to her wave, before turning and going inside.

There was no one about now, but Rose didn't mind. She'd always liked being alone. When she was little Mum used to worry about the amount of time she spent sitting up the tree in their back garden (there was only one and it was dead easy to climb). Once Rose had overheard Mum saying to Dad that they should have had another child, a little brother or sister for Rose. And Rose would have liked that, she really would, but not because she wanted someone to keep her company. She didn't mind being on her own. It gave her time to think.

She made her way past the Cloth Hall, the outline of its tower black against the stars, and turned down a side street. This part of the city was particularly quiet and Rose's footsteps sounded loud on the pavement. She passed an old-fashioned-looking café , asleep behind its peeling shutters. There was no one about, no people walking home from an evening with friends, not even any lights in the windows of the houses that lined the street. Rose felt as if she had not just the street but the whole world to herself. Then:

WHOOSH!

The noise seemed to slice through her body. A flare burst in the night sky, burning bright white for a few seconds before silently dying away. Rose stopped, her heart beating hard in her chest.

What. Was. That?

She waited for her heartbeat to go back to normal, then took a deep breath and tried to explain it to herself. It was nothing. Probably just fireworks or something.

Fireworks? said another part of her. *In February? Really?*

Well, what else could it be?

A cat flashed across the road in front of her, pausing for a second to look at her with startled eyes before disappearing up a side alley. Rose was glad to see another living creature in this lonely place. Perhaps she should go back? It was getting colder, she could feel the chill seeping through her parka. That was probably why everyone was indoors. Because it wasn't late, not even ten o'clock. And then:

BOOM.

It was a thud. A dull sound like the throb of a bass drum. It wasn't loud or close but seemed to come from somewhere deep beneath the ground. Rose felt it vibrate inside her body as she stood there, listening to her own jagged breathing.

It must be those fireworks again, she told herself.

In February? repeated the other voice.

An aeroplane, then. Traffic from a main road. Something like that.

Rose had nearly convinced herself that the strange sound wasn't strange at all when it happened again.

BOOM.

Again, she felt it rather than heard it, as if it was her own heart beating out that one dull thud.

BOOM.

Then, silence. She really would go back now, she decided, and turned to go the way she'd come.

And stopped.

Because it wasn't the way she'd come.

The brick of the buildings was dark and dirty-looking. Paint was peeling from doors and windows. There were broken cobblestones and potholes in the road and piles of rubbish in the gutters, rotting fruit and vegetables. And it didn't just look different, it *smelled* different. The air was heavy with the stink of rubbish and drains and a background trace of smoke as if something somewhere was on fire.

And it was cold now, really cold. An icy wind was stirring a faded advert on the wall. Rose huddled inside her parka and told herself not to be silly. She'd be back at the hotel in a few minutes and Grandad would laugh at her for being a scaredy cat. She'd sit in the warm restaurant with a hot chocolate in front of her and listen to Grandad and Muriel chatting together. It wasn't far, she hadn't been walking for long. She'd just take the first step and she'd be there in no time.

And then she felt something nudge against her legs.

Rose stood completely still, feeling that if she moved one inch the sky would shatter into a thousand pieces and come showering down on her in shards of blue-black glass.

Count to three, Dad used to say. *If something really scares you, close your eyes and count to three. Then take a deep breath, and you're ready to face anything.*

One. Two. Three . . . deep breath. She looked down.

It was the cat. The cat who'd run across the road a minute ago. He was entirely black, a small clot of darkness in the gloom, his yellow eyes blinking up at her as he wound around her legs, warm and soft and alive. Rose was so relieved she almost laughed. She bent down to stroke him, but before her fingers could make contact with his head something stopped her.

A whimper of fear.

Rose looked up to see a child, a little girl of about four, staring at her from the doorway of the café she'd passed. She had a grubby face and light brown hair, cut short and held back from her forehead with a green hair ribbon tied in a big bow, and she was wearing a long dress, white against the dark of the building, with a shawl around her shoulders.

Maybe she's ready for bed, thought Rose. It was late for such a little girl to be up. A flickering yellow light spilled out of the doorway behind her.

'Is it your cat?' said Rose, trying to smile. 'Does he want to go inside?'

The little girl didn't reply. She just sort of shrank into herself and carried on staring at Rose, her eyes wide. And then Rose remembered: of course, the little girl was Belgian. She couldn't understand English. She smiled again and shrugged in that theatrical way you do when you're trying to make yourself understood.

'Pussycat?' Rose pointed at the cat. 'Miaow?'

She took a step forward and the little girl screamed.

Rose stopped, horrified. What had she done to frighten the child so badly? Before she could move, a woman appeared from inside the café , speaking in rapid, angry-sounding Flemish. She too was dressed strangely, in a long dark skirt and a shawl.

'What's the matter? What are you doing?' she seemed to

be saying to the child. 'Come inside right now and—'

The angry flow of words stopped as she followed her daughter's gaze to where Rose was standing, the cat still winding around her legs.

The woman's eyes widened. It didn't seem like she could actually see Rose, not properly. She was just staring at the space Rose was occupying, as if Rose – like the cat – was a clot of darkness, a Rose-shaped black hole in the night. The mother grabbed her child's hand, her eyes never leaving the place where Rose was standing.

Rose said, 'I'm sorry. I frightened your little girl. I'm English. I didn't mean—'

The woman let loose another stream of furious, frightened words, then pulled the girl inside and slammed the door. The light above the door went out and all was quiet.

Rose was alone with the cat. He blinked at her again, then turned and stalked off down the alleyway, tail in the air as if he'd accomplished something important. Somewhere, a dog started to bark. Then, almost imperceptibly, a faint sound of music filtered through the blue-black darkness. It was a band Rose recognised, a reassuringly familiar noise that sounded as if it was coming from a bar. The night was coming back into focus. Rose felt drizzle on her face and could make out the outline of the Cloth Hall tower pointing up against the sky.

She set off, back the way she'd come, putting one foot in front of the other, refusing to let herself hurry. The street was familiar now. She saw a concert poster she'd passed before, and a scrawl of graffiti. A plastic carrier bag blew in the wind. As the sights and sounds of the familiar world seeped back through the darkness, she forced herself to walk normally.

But as she got closer to the hotel and could see the glow of the lights in the not-square square, she started to run. Whatever had happened in that little side street was behind her. And she wanted it to stay that way.

By the time Rose burst into the hotel, her cheeks were hot and she was seriously out of breath. Grandad made a big show of looking at his watch.

'Fourteen and a half minutes precisely,' he said. 'You just made it.'

He and Muriel were sitting at a table at the back of the empty restaurant, drinking something out of tiny glasses, and soon Rose was with them, a hot chocolate in front of her, just as she'd imagined, listening to their gentle laughter. What had happened out there in the night – the light in the sky, the boom, the strange street, the terrified little girl – it all seemed like it had happened to someone else.

Maybe it hadn't happened at all.

Grandad was watching her over the top of his glasses. 'You all right, Cabbage? You look a bit hot and bothered. Not coming down with something, I hope?'

Rose brought her hands up to her cheeks. They felt like they were on fire. 'I'm fine, Grandad. I ran part of the way back, that's all.'

'Why? Was someone chasing you?' They all laughed.

'I told you, Brian,' said Muriel. 'Ieper is a very safe place.'

Then it was bedtime. They said their goodnights and went up the stairs. Rose was reassured by the sight of her bright neat bedroom at the top of the building. Her face in the mirror as she cleaned her teeth was the same old face: dark eyes, straight nose with a sprinkle of freckles, frizzy hair which she'd straighten again tomorrow. Nothing had changed.

She got out her phone to text Dad, then stopped, staring at the screen. She still didn't know what to say. She couldn't tell him about what had just happened. It was too weird, too confusing. So she just plugged her phone into the charger and got into bed.

Even with the bedside light off the room wasn't completely dark. Rose closed her eyes. And slept . . .

She never knew whether it was hours or just minutes later that she woke. But she did know one thing: she heard them first in a dream. Weary male voices, singing in time with marching feet.

'I wonder who's kissing her now . . .'

The dream didn't stop when Rose opened her eyes. Everything looked the same, but the voices were still there. In the room with her. She reached for the bedside light, wondering if she was still dreaming. The room sprang into light, bright and modern and clean. But she could still hear the voices and the tramp of boots on stone, each step sounding like an effort.

'One, two, three, four . . . One, two, three, four . . .'

And then Rose realised: they weren't in the room, how could they be?

They were outside in the square.

She got out of bed. Her bare feet felt freezing in spite of the carpet and a bit of grit got stuck to the bottom of one of them. *Why is it so cold?* she wondered. Of course, the heating must've been turned off for the night.

She moved over to the window and looked out.

The square was deserted. It looked just the same as it did before: modern street lights, a few parked cars, the cobblestones wet with rain . . .

And it was silent. The song had stopped.

It all looked so utterly ordinary in the orange glow of the street lights that Rose wondered if she'd imagined it all: the girl's voice in her room; the photo that disappeared from her phone; the flares and booms in the night sky; the terrified child – and now this. The men singing, the tramp of their marching feet . . .

She stared out at the empty square. And then, just as she'd decided to forget it and go back to bed, something scratched at the door.

Scratch. Scratch. Scratch-scratch-scratch.

Every drop of blood in Rose's body seemed to freeze. She tried to turn but found she couldn't move.

Scratch. Scratch-scratch. Scratch-scratch.

Whatever was out there *really* wanted to come in.

One. Two. Three.

Deep breath.

Slowly, very slowly, she turned and walked across the room. The floor felt like a trampoline beneath her feet. She grasped the handle, the metal chilly beneath her fingers, and opened the door.

It was the dog. The dog who'd been waiting for them when they arrived at the station, and then at the hotel, was standing outside the door, wagging his tail and looking just as normal and cheerful and doggy as ever. Rose didn't care how he'd got into the hotel, or what he was doing there. She was just pleased to see him.

The dog seemed pleased to see Rose too. He gave a polite little wuff of recognition, then turned and ran off down the dark landing, his claws clicking against the floorboards.

The floorboards.

But the floor on the landing was carpeted, like her bedroom. Wasn't it?

She looked down. Beneath her bare feet was dark polished wood, like the floor downstairs in the lobby.

'Wuff!'

The dog waited till she looked up at him and then ran off up the stairs.

Up. The stairs.

Up . . .

Rose's room was on the top floor. There *were* no stairs going up. She was at the top of the building. But there they were. The stairs, a narrow flight, uncarpeted, with a wooden handrail, heading up.

To where? Where did they go?

Rose ducked back into her room, shoved her feet into her boots, and then ran after the dog up the stairs that didn't exist into the darkness at the top. She could just see him waiting for her on the landing, looking expectantly at a closed door. It was clear he wanted to go in.

She put a hand on the doorknob. It was wooden, not cold to the touch like the metal one downstairs. The door swung open and Rose followed the dog inside.

It was a small room, smaller even than Rose's, full of disorder and moonlight. The single bed was unmade and there was a half-packed suitcase open on the floor. Clothes were spilling out of a small chest of drawers against the wall. A pair of lace-up boots had been left lying by the bed, and a long dark coat hung on a hook on the back of the door.

For a moment, Rose just stood there, trying to take it all in. What was this place? What was going on?

She bent down to pick up a picture that had fallen off the chest and was lying face down on the floor. The face of a young man in uniform stared back at her from behind the broken glass. Another of those sad-eyed wartime faces. She placed the picture carefully back on the chest and shivered. It was freezing – and no wonder. The window was wide open, the curtains blowing in an icy wind, and there was snow on the floor.

And then she heard them again:

'I wonder who's kissing her now . . .'

The men's voices swelled, filling the darkness. The singing was louder up here. More real.

Rose moved across the room as if an invisible thread was pulling her to the window. She seemed to have no choice.

The square was familiar in the moonlight, but the misty drizzle had disappeared and now snowflakes were swirling through the darkness and whitening the cobblestones.

But that wasn't all. Because *they* were there. The soldiers. A hundred of them, maybe two hundred, marching four abreast, hunched in their khaki uniforms, packs on their backs, rifles over their shoulders, tramping through the snow, singing their bittersweet song of longing and regret.

Rose stared. For one mad moment she thought it was maybe some parade, a historical re-enactment, a film was being made . . .

And then she thought, *In the middle of the night? With no one else there? And what about the snow? And the fact that I'm watching from a room that doesn't actually exist?*

As Rose watched them, it felt like she and the soldiers were the only people in the world. Yet none of them saw her. Not a single one looked up. They just marched on, eyes front, weary, focused on getting wherever they had to be. To them, Rose didn't exist.

And then she saw him, at the very back of the line. He was smaller than the others, skinny and marching slightly out of time with a little skip in his step. And in his button-hole was a bunch of yellow flowers, like the ones she'd picked from the bank of the canal. What did Grandad say they were called? Celandines, that was it. She'd left some on the boy soldier's grave.

And then he looked up.

He did.

He looked up and he saw Rose. Their eyes met, and for a brief moment everything seemed to stop. The snowflakes froze in the air and the stars held their breath. Then the boy grinned, a cheeky, familiar grin as if he'd known her all his life, and the picture broke up and time moved on. The boy touched his cap with one finger in a little salute and hurried after the others, with his strange skipping march.

For a second, Rose just stood there. Something had happened. She didn't know what it was, but she had to find out. She grabbed the coat from behind the door and ran out of the room, pausing only to look back at the dog.

'Coming?' she said.

'Wuff!' He wagged his tail and followed her down the stairs, his claws clicking on the floorboards.

7

It was dark on the staircase, so dark that Rose had to inch her way down, putting out one foot at a time to feel for the next step and keeping tight hold of the banister. She could feel her heart thudding in her ears, but it was more from excitement than fear. What was she going to find when she reached the square? Who were those men?

Who was that boy?

When she reached the first landing, Rose felt around for a light switch. The wall was rough under her hand and she couldn't find a switch. It was probably just as well, she thought, she didn't want to wake anyone. She made it to the bottom at last, reassured by the clicking of the dog's claws on the stairs behind her. It wasn't quite so dark down here. Moonlight was shining though the semi-circular window above the front door, filling the room with greyness and shadows and, as Rose stumbled to the door, she could hear the grandfather clock ticking in the dark.

The dog watched as she fumbled with the iron latch. The door wasn't locked. That surprised her. She would've thought Muriel was the kind of person to be extra careful about things like that. But maybe Ypres was the kind of place where no one ever locked their doors. Muriel did say it was very safe.

The door swung open easily when she pulled it, letting a gust of snow-speckled moonlight into the hall.

Here goes, Rose thought.

She hugged the unfamiliar coat around herself, catching a faint dusty whiff of Parma violets, the previous owner's perfume perhaps. It reminded Rose of the old-fashioned chalky sweets Dad used to buy her from their local corner shop. Then, the dog at her heels, she stepped out into the square.

The cold took her breath away. The icy wind pulled at her hair, spattering her face with snowflakes that stung like sand.

'Wuff!' The dog was looking up at her.

'What's going on?' she asked him. 'What's happening?'

He wagged his tail and then – to Rose's horror – turned and scampered off into the snow.

'Where are you going?' she called. 'Come back! Don't leave me!'

But he was gone, leaving Rose standing there alone, with the snow whirling around her. The square was deserted. There were no lights in any of the buildings, no sounds, no sign of the soldiers. Had she left her nice warm bed and come out in the middle of the night wearing nothing but her pyjamas and a manky old coat because of some stupid dream?

But if it was a dream, where did the coat come from?

And the room? Rooms didn't just appear from nowhere. And then there was the snow.

What about the snow?

Rose turned her face up to the whirling snowflakes and breathed in the familiar smell of ice and winter. There was something else as well: a dark smell that was faint and powerful at the same time. It made Rose think of autumn and Bonfire Night and the sound of rockets screeching up over the London rooftops and exploding like giant fiery flowers.

And then she realised: the smell was charred wood. Something had been burnt here recently, something big. She looked around, wondering what it was, but couldn't see much through the whirling whiteness. And then she looked down. She didn't know why she hadn't done it before, because there at her feet was the proof she wasn't dreaming.

Footprints.

The snow had been churned up by hundreds of feet. So they had been here, the soldiers. They were real. Which meant *he* was real too, the boy she'd seen from the window.

And then she heard the noise. It was faint at first, so faint that she felt it rather than heard it, a vibration in the air, a weird fluttering, then whooshing sound. It was getting louder. And closer.

'*Look out!*'

A body, coming from nowhere, hitting her like a train, pushing her backwards so she crashed on to her back, head smashing on the cobblestones, the sweet metallic taste of blood in her mouth, the other body falling flat on top of hers, crushing her . . .

And then, the explosion.

The loudest thing she'd ever heard. Rose felt the world spinning around her and the ground shuddering beneath her and, after a tiny second of silence, debris coming down like rain.

The loudest noise now was the pounding of her heart. That must mean she wasn't dead, musn't it?

She became conscious of some scratchy fabric against her cheek and the fact that her head hurt where it had hit the pavement. There was a smell of wool and oil and sweat. A slight trace of peppermint. No, she wasn't dead. Just flat on her back in the snow with someone lying on top of her.

'Blimey,' the someone said. 'That was a close one.'

It was a boy's voice with a slight croak and a strange accent that sounded a bit like London but wasn't. Rose realised her eyes were shut. She opened them and found herself looking into a pair of bright brown eyes.

'Hello,' said the owner of the eyes. He didn't seem at all embarrassed by the fact that his face was literally an inch away from hers. 'I forgot you was there for a tick. Old whizz-bang took me mind clean off it.'

'Ow?' said Rose. She didn't know what else to say.

The boy grinned. There was a gap between his front teeth. 'You're not dead, then?'

'Don't think so.'

'Nor me. Just as well, eh?'

Rose was in too much pain to feel embarrassed. 'I'm a bit squashed. Can you—?'

'What? Oh yeah. Sorry. Sorry, sorry.'

He scrambled to his feet and, before Rose had a chance to get up, stood there, silhouetted against the whirling snowflakes, looking down at her.

'Angel in the snow.'

'What?' Rose was struggling to get up now.

'Didn't you never do that when you was a kiddie?'

Before Rose could reply, he lay down on his back in some fresh snow, spread out his arms and moved them up and down.

'What are you—?'

'Shh! You'll see.' He got up carefully, leaving behind the outline of his body, and pointed to the shapes he'd made with his arms. 'See? Angel wings! Like an angel's been lying there. I can't believe you never done that.'

Rose looked down at the shape in the snow. It was like the outline of an angel. Then she looked at the boy. He was small – not much taller than her – and skinny, dressed in the heavy khaki uniform of a British soldier. And in his buttonhole was a bunch of little yellow flowers, now very crushed.

'It's you,' she said.

The boy glanced over his shoulder, pretending there was someone else there, then pointed at himself. 'Is it?' he said. 'I s'pose it must be. Large as life and twice as much trouble, as my Aunty Dot would say.'

'I saw you. With the other soldiers. From up there.' The snow was easing off now and you could see the tiny attic window quite clearly.

'You did,' said the boy. 'And I saw you. Looking down at me like a little star in the sky.' He twinkled at her, as if he was a star himself. 'And what I want to know is, what the heck made you come out in the middle of a raid?'

Rose's stomach felt suddenly hollow. 'A raid?' she said. 'What d'you mean?'

'Well, it wasn't a vicarage tea party, was it?'

Rose shivered. What was going on?

'Chilly?' said the boy. 'You want my jacket?'

'No. I'm all right. Thank you.'

'Course you are. Angels don't feel the cold, do they?'

As he looked at her, Rose felt very glad of her borrowed coat. Not because it was warm (though it was), but because it was long and hid every inch of her pyjamas. She'd had them since she was twelve and they were covered in owls. Green owls.

The boy sighed and looked at the sky. 'Speaking of raids, we should get away from here,' he said. 'Blighters always aim for the clock tower – 'scuse my French – you can see it for miles.'

'But . . .' Rose looked at the hotel behind them. 'I should really get back,' she said. 'My grandad—'

'We need to go. Trust me.'

And she did. Rose didn't know why, but there was something about this boy that she did trust. She didn't know who he was or where he'd come from. But somehow he made her feel – *comfortable*. She usually felt awkward with boys, especially ones she liked. She had often discussed it with Grace and Ella, all three of them wondering why they couldn't talk to boys in the same way they talked to each other. But Rose didn't feel like that with this boy. She felt as if she'd known him for ever, but at the same time she was excited, because they'd only just met.

Most of all, in spite of all the weirdness, she felt – *happy*. She was out in the snow in the middle of the night with a boy – a boy who didn't make her feel embarrassed or wish she was someone else. He just made her feel like herself. So if this was a dream, Rose didn't want to wake up. Not yet, anyway.

'It doesn't look like I've got much choice, does it?' she said, smiling at him.

He grinned back, his eyes dancing around her face. 'No, sweet, it don't. Come on.'

He held out his hand. After a moment's hesitation, she took it and they set off. Halfway across the square, Rose felt a bit awkward holding the hand of a complete stranger so she took her hand away and thrust it into the pocket of her borrowed coat. Inside there was a button and a screwed-up handkerchief.

'You're English,' the boy said, looking at her from the corner of his eyes.

'So are you.'

'That is true, but to be expected. Whereas you—'

'What about me?'

'I thought you was a local girl when I saw you sitting up there in your attic. A servant or something. Maid, you know. Not *English*, not an *English* girl. What you doing here?'

Rose didn't know what to say, so she told him the truth. 'I'm here with my grandad.'

'With your *grandad*?' The boy looked astonished.

But before she could reply there was a scrabble of claws and a flurry of snow as a white shape shot past them in pursuit of a smaller, darker shape.

'Oi! Leave poor pussycat alone, you bully!'

Rose's heart leapt. It was the dog, she was sure of it. *Her* dog. 'Hey!' she called after him. 'Come back!' But he'd disappeared into the darkness. 'I've seen that dog before,' she said.

'There's a lot of them about,' said the boy. 'People had to leave them behind when they went, you know, the local people. Left them running around the streets, nowhere to go.'

Rose was outraged. 'That's awful!'

'I know,' he replied. 'I don't like to see an animal with no home to go to neither. Still, what could they do? Look, there he is.'

They had arrived at a place which looked vaguely familiar where the street passed through a gap in the city walls. The dog was sitting in the snow with his back to them, staring at the wall.

'What have you done with poor pussycat, matey?' said the boy. 'We could do with him down the barracks, nice big cat like that.' He looked at Rose. 'Rats, you see. Crawling with them, it is.'

Rose remembered a song Grandad used to sing when she was little. She sang a snatch of it:

'Rats, rats, big as pussycats—'

The boy joined in: 'In the stores, in the stores . . .'

They looked at each other and laughed.

'You know that one, do you?' he said. 'Our rats are bigger than pussycats, as it happens. Horrible things.' He did a little mime of firing a rifle. 'Boom. Where'd puss go? Come on, chum, out the way.'

'What are you doing?' said Rose, crouching down by the dog and scratching his ears.

'Going to catch old puss. Take him down the barracks. Like a mascot or something. Keep the rats down.' The boy squatted down beside the ancient rampart. 'He's gone in here, found himself a hidey-hole.' He pointed to a gap among the stones. ' Come on, puss, come to Joe.'

Joe? He was called Joe?

It was a common enough name, there were two or three

Joes in Rose's year at school, but even so . . .

'Keep hold of the dog, will you, angel? Don't want him scaring puss away.'

'What? Oh, yes. Yes.' Rose held on to the dog, her fingers in his rough coat, as the boy – as *Joe* – peered into the hole in the wall.

'Goes back quite a way. Come on, puss. I know . . .' He rummaged in his pocket and brought something out. 'Look at this, lovely bit of biscuit. Out you come.'

'He won't come. Not for that.'

'He will. I've got a way with animals. That's it, mate. Come on. See?'

As the cat emerged from the hole in the wall, the dog went mad, slithered out of Rose's arms and launched himself at him. The cat rocketed off down the road, with the dog after him. Joe stood up and watched them disappear into the night.

'Oh well. It was worth a try.'

He turned back to Rose with a grin. It had stopped snowing now and the moon was shining, bleaching the colour from the world and making it look like a black-and-white photograph. The grin faded as his eyes rested on her.

'Look at you. Standing there in the moonlight.'

If anyone else had said it, Rose would've felt embarrassed. Especially if they were looking at her the way he was. But with this boy it was different. She didn't feel embarrassed at all. She felt special.

He didn't take his eyes from her face. 'Where did you come from?' He sounded puzzled, but also grateful, as if someone had just given him the most amazing present.

Rose shrugged. What could she say? She couldn't explain what she was doing there. She didn't know herself.

'I – don't know.'

'What? You must know where you come from.'

'I thought I did, but . . .'

'You've got to have a name, though. I can't keep calling you angel.'

'It's Rose.'

The boy sighed as if he was pleased with the information. 'Of course it is. Of course! You're a rose in no man's land.'

'What?'

'It's another song. You don't know that one?'

Rose shook her head.

He sang, posing as if he was onstage: *'"There's a rose that grows in no man's land–"'* He stopped. 'I'd sing you the rest, but I don't want to scare you away.'

Rose laughed. It was true. She did feel like she was in some sort of no man's land.

The boy held out his right hand. 'How d'you do, Rose? I'm Joe.'

Rose took his hand and for a moment they stood there in the moonlight looking at each other. 'Hello, Joe.'

'It's my birthday tomorrow,' he said, releasing her hand and throwing her a sneaky look.

Rose caught her breath. He was called Joe and his birthday was on Valentine's Day? 'February the fourteenth?' she said. She couldn't believe it.

'Not just a pretty face, are you, Rose?' No one had ever called Rose pretty before. Well, except for Mum and Dad, but that didn't count. 'Yup, same day every year. Comes around like clockwork. Tick tock, tick tock.'

'Valentine's Day . . .'

'That's right. You can't say no to me now, can you?'

It's a coincidence, thought Rose. *It has to be.* She shook the thought away. 'Depends what you're asking.'

'Ah ha! I'm asking you to join me for a bite to eat at a little estaminet what I happen to know in the vicinity. It ain't far and they do a cracking egg and chips.'

Was he asking her out? Like – *on a date?*

Rose had often thought about this moment , talked about it with Grace and Ella: what you'd say when someone asked you out. If you didn't like them, how would you say no without hurting their feelings, and if you did like them, how would you say yes without looking too keen? And it was funny, because now it had happened she knew exactly what to say. She said:

'All right.'

'All right!'

Joe held out his hand. Rose took it and they walked down the street together, leaving a trail of footprints behind them in the fresh snow.

8

As they turned into the little side street, picking their way across broken pavements and slithering in the snow, Rose began to feel she'd been there before.

'There she is,' said Joe. 'The finest estaminet in town. Well, the only one open this late.'

There was a window lit by a single flickering candle. And now Rose realised where they were. It was the street she'd walked down when she'd gone off on her own after dinner with Grandad. The street where she'd seen the little girl in the doorway of the café .

'Look at it,' Joe went on. 'The light of the world, shining in the darkness, calling out to us, "Egg and chips . . . come and get my egg and chips . . ."'

Rose giggled. 'It's a caff,' she said.

And it was the same café , she saw that now. But something had happened since she was last there. The shutters were open, and the windowpanes were broken. There was rubble on the pavement outside.

'Call it what you want, sweet,' said Joe. 'Long as it's got a bit of a roof and serves hot grub, it's good enough for me.'

As he made for the door, Rose stopped him. 'I've been here before,' she said. 'What happened to the window?'

Joe shrugged. 'Caught the force of a blast, by the looks of it.'

He held the door for her, and she stepped inside. The café was a tiny place with only a couple of tables and a small counter at the back. It was just as cold inside as it was in the street and there was snow on the floor that had blown in through the broken window. Joe made for the table furthest from the door and pulled out a chair for Rose. They were the only customers.

'Egg and chips, m'lady?' said Joe.

'I'm not hungry, thanks.' She was still full of the pizza she'd had earlier.

'Sure? Well, you'll just have to watch me eat. Not a pretty sight. *Bong jour*?' he called out. 'Madame?'

Rose waited, wondering if the same woman would appear, the mother of the little girl who'd been so frightened of her. But it was an elderly woman who emerged from the back room. She was dressed entirely in black and wore a scarf over her hair.

'*Erfs?*' said Joe. He used the same voice that Grandad did when he was talking to foreigners. 'Chips? Bee-er?'

The old woman nodded and said something in Flemish.

'*Merci,*' added Joe as she trudged away. He pronounced it 'mercy'.

'They don't speak French here, you know,' said Rose.

'Neither do I, so that's all right.' He grinned at her across the table. 'Poor old soul, she ought to get out while she can.

75

A lot of the people have gone already.'

'Gone?' said Rose. 'Gone where?'

He shrugged. 'Dunno. France, I think. Holland? Some to England. Where you from?'

'London.'

'London! Straight up? You'll be looking down your nose at me then. Dorking,' he added in answer to her unspoken question.

'I've never been there.'

'You don't want to. Well, you do now, of course. You'll be coming to see me when we get back.'

Rose raised her eyebrows. 'You reckon?'

'I reckon.'

He was very sure of himself, this boy. But Rose didn't mind. She quite liked it, in fact.

'I'll show you all the sights,' he continued. 'The horse trough. The duck pond. The coal yard.'

'Sounds exciting.'

'It do, don't it? It's not, though. It's the most boring town ever. That's why I joined up.'

'Joined up?'

He patted his uniform. 'The army, you know. Your country needs you, all that guff? I'm one of Kitchener's boys.'

That was just ridiculous. Rose couldn't believe it. 'You joined the army because you were *bored*?'

'Why not? Me and my two best pals went along to the recruiting office. We reckoned it'd be a laugh. Better than staying at home anyway. In *Dorking*.'

'What did your mum say?'

'Mother? Lor', what didn't she say?' Joe rolled his eyes. 'She shouted, cried, threw a scrubbing brush at me head, shouted again. Cried again. Got over it in the end, though. Give me this.' He reached in his pocket.

'What is it?'

'Her lucky sixpence.'

He put it on the table. It was an old silver coin with a hole roughly drilled through the middle. A leather thong had been threaded through the hole. Rose picked it up by the thong and held it up in the candlelight. The markings on the coin were nearly worn away.

'It belonged to her dad,' Joe was saying. 'He was in South Africa, fighting the Boers, and it brought him back in one piece. So Mum reckoned it'd bring me back in one piece an' all.'

'So now it's your lucky sixpence.'

'Yeah, I suppose it is. Ah, here we go, grub up.'

The old woman came out with a plate of food and a glass of light-coloured beer. She put them down in front of Joe, who paid her with a handful of change. 'Mercy!' he called after her retreating back then started on his meal, wolfing it down as if he hadn't eaten for days. He paused, looking at Rose over a forkful of fried egg.

'Sure you don't wish to partake, m'lady?'

'So sure.'

He waggled a chip at her. 'Go on. It's trez beans, you know.'

'What?' Rose looked at him. 'What did you just say? Trez—?'

'Beans.' He grinned and ate the chip himself. 'Trez beans. I was lying before, wasn't I, when I said I couldn't speak French.'

Rose laughed. 'Oh, I get it! Trè s bien! "Very good"!'

'Oooh! Hark at you with your frenchifiediness!' He

looked across at her, the grin fading from his face. 'What did you say you was doing here, Rose?'

'I didn't.'

'No, you didn't, did you. How old are you?'

'Fourteen.'

'Fourteen?' Joe looked as if he was going to say something, but changed his mind. 'Bit young to be wandering the streets of a strange city by yourself, ain't you?'

'You can talk.'

The words slipped out before Rose could stop them. Joe paused, his fork halfway to his mouth.

'What d'you mean?'

'It's your birthday tomorrow, yeah?'

'That's what I said.'

'Valentine's Day.'

'So? You going to give me a birthday kiss?' His bright brown eyes danced around her face. 'When I've finished me egg and chips, of course.'

He went back to his enthusiastic food shovelling. Rose watched him for a minute.

'So how old are you going to be?' she said.

Joe looked up from his food. There was a moment's pause before he replied.

'Twenty,' he said. Rose detected a note of challenge in his voice, as if he was expecting to be contradicted.

She put her head on one side. '*Really?*' she said. There was no way this boy was nineteen.

'Cross my heart, Rose. I would say hope to die, but that might be tempting fate.' He pulled a face. 'Any more questions, m'lady?'

'Just one.' Rose took a deep breath. 'Is that your only name? Joe? Your only first name, I mean.'

Joe put down his fork. 'Have you been spying, Rose? Did my mum send you to keep an eye on me?'

She shook her head. 'No. It's just—'

'JOE!'

She was interrupted by a shout from the doorway. Two young men in khaki were standing there, grinning.

'Thought we'd find you here!'

'What you been up to, you dog? Met some young mamselle, did you?'

'Chuck it, Fred,' said Joe, glancing at Rose. She looked away, suddenly feeling shy. 'Just having a bite to eat, boys. You know how it is.'

'Well, you'd best get a move on, chum,' said the dark-haired boy. He was taller than the other. 'We're due back at ten and we'll be for it if we're late.'

Joe looked at the clock on the wall. It was ten to ten. Cowboy time, Dad always used to call it.

'Oh, lor',' he said, looking down at his half-finished meal.

'You coming?'

'You go ahead, Tonk,' said Joe. 'I'll be right behind you.'

'You'd best be.'

Joe bolted down the rest of his food as his friends left the café . 'You be all right if I leave you here, Rose? It'll be jankers for me if I'm late. Can't risk it.'

'I'll be fine,' she replied, although she had no idea whether she would be.

'Yeah, I think you will, actually. There's something about you.' He got up and wiped his mouth on his khaki sleeve. 'Will I see you again, Rose?'

'I don't know.' She really didn't.

Joe held her gaze for a minute, then broke the moment with a little shake of his head. 'Yeah, I'll see you again. And next time I'll have that kiss off you. Hey, look at that.' He nodded towards the back of the café . 'Someone else has took a fancy to you, Rose.'

It was the same little girl, the one with the grubby face and the green hair ribbon that Rose had seen when she went off on her own after the pizza with Grandad. And then, just like before, the child's mother appeared and pulled her daughter away into the back room, all the time casting frightened glances at the chair where Rose was sitting.

Joe laughed. 'Seems like it's past someone's bedtime.' He looked at the clock again. 'Mine too. Scc you, Rose. Next time.'

He gave her his little salute – one finger touching the cap – just like he'd done when she'd watched him from the window of the hotel. Then the door shut and he was gone. Rose was alone in the empty café , staring at his empty plate, smeared yellow from the eggs. His plate, his glass and – his lucky sixpence, the one his mum had given him. He'd left it on the table.

'Joe!'

Rose grabbed the sixpence and jumped to her feet. It suddenly seemed terribly important to get it back to him. She ran to the door.

But when she opened it and looked out there was no sign of Joe or his friends.

The world had changed again.

9

Sunlight. That was the first thing. It wasn't dark any more, or cold. The snow had gone and the sun felt warm on Rose's face, although there was still slush on her boots. She blinked, dazzled for a minute, then as her eyes adjusted from the dim light inside the café , she looked around, unable to believe her eyes.

It wasn't just the time of day that had changed, or the season. The city had changed too. The street which, moments ago, had only one or two buildings missing, like gaps in a smile, was now devastated. It wasn't even a street any more, just heaps of rubble with a few walls still standing. There was a large shell hole by Rose's feet, half full of oily rainwater that glinted blue and purple in the sun like the back of a beetle. Somewhere, a baby was crying.

With a growing sense of panic, Rose turned to look back at the little café where she'd just been sitting, watching Joe eat egg and chips.

It was gone.

There was nothing there. Just a heap of bricks and broken glass. The back wall was still there, but the doorway through which the old woman had brought Joe's meal was a gaping hole. Beyond it, Rose could see the remains of her kitchen: a smashed stove, broken furniture, saucepans on the floor. What had happened to the old woman? she wondered. To the mother? To the little girl with the green hair ribbon?

Rose shut her eyes, screwing up her face like a little girl herself, and wished to be back in bed in her room at the top of the hotel with her grandad asleep downstairs. It was a dream, she told herself. It had to be. She'd seen the grave of the boy soldier, Joe – *Valentine Joe* – and she'd got upset. Mum always said she was too sensitive. Silly things made her cry: a lost spider, a lonely teddy bear in a shop window. And that was what was happening now. She'd felt so sad and sorry and helpless about the boy being killed that now she was dreaming about him, dreaming she'd met him. Dreaming she could help him, even. But it wasn't really happening, of course it wasn't. And when she opened her eyes it would be over.

She opened her eyes.

It wasn't over. Nothing had changed. It was all still there. The sunshine, the shattered street, the baby crying. It was real.

And Rose was part of it. Whatever it was, wherever it was, *when*ever it was, she was there and she didn't know whether she could ever get back, to Grandad, to London.

To Mum.

She didn't know what to do at all.

As Rose stood there, helpless among the ruins, a woman hurried past, skirting around the edges of the shell hole.

She was dragging a child by the hand, a little boy who was hanging back and complaining. As they passed, the boy stared at Rose, looking back at her over his shoulder, until his mother jerked him on.

The woman didn't seem to see Rose at all.

As she watched them go, Rose became conscious of something clenched in her fist. She unfurled her fingers. Of course. It was Joe's lucky sixpence, the one his mum had given him, warm from the heat of Rose's hand. As she looked at it Rose knew what she had to do. She must find Joe and give it back to him. But where was he? Was he still in the city? Was he even still alive?

A figure emerged from a side street up ahead. It was a young soldier, not very tall, a bit skinny, sauntering after the woman, hands in his pockets, as if he had all the time in the world. Joe?

'Joe!'

He kicked a small stone, catching it on the toe of his boot, then flicking it up in the air.

'Joe!'

He was too far away to hear. Rose started to run, stumbling around the edge of the shell hole, skidding on the loose stones.

'JOE!'

She was just behind him now, nearly close enough to touch.

'I've got your lucky sixpence, Joe. You left it in the—'

Then, another voice, behind her:

'Bert?'

Rose spun round. Behind her, two more soldiers had emerged from the side street and were calling after their mate.

'Albert! Hold your horses!'

The young soldier ahead of Rose turned to face his mates. He wasn't a bit like Joe. He had ginger curls sticking out from under his cap. Rose was so close to him that she could see his freckles and feel his breath on her face.

But he looked straight through her as if she wasn't there.

'What's your hurry?' he called, as his friends ran up to join him, boots pounding on the stones.

Rose was surrounded. She felt trapped, like on a tube train at rush hour. They were close enough to touch, too close – she could smell them: the greasy scent of unwashed male hair and stale woollen uniforms. But they had no idea she was there.

'Got to get back to barracks,' said one friend.

'We've got the call,' said the other.

'No!'

'Yes! We're off to the Front, boys!'

Rose looked from one face to another as the young men laughed and slapped each other's backs, as excited as schoolboys who'd won a football game. Then they moved off together, jumping and stumbling over the rubble, up the ruined street.

Rose followed them. She didn't know what else to do.

Unlike the little side street where she'd sat in the café with Joe, the city square was heaving with activity. There was a smell of petrol, the sound of hooves on cobblestones and all sorts of vehicles: army lorries, what seemed to be ambulances with red crosses on their sides, wagons and horses, even a couple of old-fashioned London buses still with their advertisements for Pears' Soap and PG Tips. The great Cloth Hall was gone. All that was left was part of its clock tower sticking up against the blue of the sky like a broken finger.

'Quick march!'

A battalion of Sikh soldiers wearing khaki turbans was on the move, marching behind an officer on horseback, heading out of the square. Rose wondered how many of their names would end up engraved on the cold white marble of the Menin Gate and be photographed by a schoolboy with an iPhone a hundred years from now.

That was when the truth hit her.

She'd known it for some time, deep down, what was happening, but she hadn't accepted it. It was too big, too incredible, too terrifying.

Until now. Now she *knew* it was true.

She'd wanted to be in the past, to be with her dad again, and now she was. But this wasn't her dad's time. It was ages before that, the years of the First World War. She didn't know how it had happened, or why, but somehow (the thought buzzed in her brain like a bluebottle against a window), somehow she knew it had something to with Joe. Valentine Joe Strudwick, the boy soldier whose grave she'd seen. Maybe she'd been sent back to help him? To save him?

Was that even possible?

A steady stream of civilians was trudging past the Sikh soldiers towards the other end of the square. There were women carrying babies, their faces set and defiant. Children leading smaller children. Weary-looking old men pushing bicycles, prams loaded with a few sad possessions. There were animals, too: a mule pulling a loaded wagon with a little boy perched precariously on top; two children in a little cart pulled by a big dog; an old man leading a donkey; a boy with a cow on a piece of rope.

The remaining citizens of Ypres were on the move, leaving their city because it was no longer safe for them to be there. Some, mostly women with young children, were being organised into military vehicles by a group of soldiers wearing khaki kilts.

Rose looked across at the hotel where she'd gone to bed a few hours before. It seemed like a different life, with a different Rose drifting through it as if in a dream. She found herself wondering if she'd ever get back to that life, then quickly pushed the thought away. What mattered now, mattered more than anything had ever mattered before, was to find Joe and give him back his lucky sixpence.

She felt it in the pocket of her borrowed coat and pushed another awful thought to the back of her mind: she'd seen his grave. What if he died *because* he'd lost his lucky sixpence? Because she, Rose, hadn't been able to find him and give it back to him?

What if he was killed because of her?

She set off, slipping through the crowds like a ghost, looking into the faces of the soldiers as she passed. None of them was Joe. And no one saw her. No one knew she was there. Only the children looked at her, staring back over their shoulders as their mothers trudged past. Then, just as Rose was beginning to despair, she saw a face she recognised. Two faces, in fact, amongst a group of soldiers lounging in the sun near the ruined Cloth Hall.

'Fred?'

He was with Joe's other friend, Tonk, telling him something that was making him laugh.

'Tonk?' Rose hurried over to them. 'I've got to find Joe.' She felt the sixpence in the pocket of her borrowed coat. 'Please!'

She was nearly shouting now, but no one heard her except a horse who shied away in alarm. In desperation, she grabbed Tonk's arm. She could feel the rough cloth of his sleeve beneath her fingers but all he did was twitch his arm as if a fly had landed on it. Then he shuddered.

Fred looked at him. 'You all right, chum? Not coming down with something, are you?'

Tonk grinned. 'Nah, mate, I'm fine. Ghost walked over my grave.'

As Rose stared at him, startled by his use of Grandad's phrase, a lorry passed behind him, loaded with wooden crosses.

'Where's Joe anyway?' Tonk continued. 'Haven't seen him for a while.'

Rose's heart leapt. So he was alive.

Fred shook his head. 'Who knows? Canoodling with that imaginary sweetheart of his, I expect. Come on.'

They got up, laughing together in the pale spring sunshine. Rose stood and watched them go as the people surged around her.

'Wuff?'

That same small polite bark which meant, 'Excuse me, but I'm here and I would like your attention, please.'

The dog was looking up at her, wagging his tail, like he was just waiting for his evening walk. Rose felt a surge of relief as she bent down and buried her face in his coarse fur, breathing in his dry doggy smell. If he was here, things couldn't be as bad as all that.

Could they?

10

'Take cover!'

The shout went up from one of the soldiers. No one needed to be told twice. Women grabbed their children, soldiers threw themselves to the ground, those that could run, ran.

And the dog bolted.

'Wait!' Rose sprinted after him across the square, dodging the frightened people and crying children and the rearing, rolling-eyed horses. '*Wait!*'

He was heading towards the hotel. Rose's hotel, the one where, in another life, another Rose was staying with her grandad.

'Not in there!'

Too late. He'd dodged in through the open doorway. Rose heard the sinister fluttering, whooshing sound she'd heard before, and didn't hesitate. She dived in after the dog as the square exploded.

*

Rose was woken, she didn't know how much later, by something nuzzling her face. She opened her eyes. She was lying on the floor, near where the reception desk had been when she and Grandad had checked in. She could see the grandfather clock (could it be the same one?) standing against the wall, but couldn't hear its tick. The dog was standing over her, managing to look worried and cheerful at the same time. There was smoke everywhere and debris all over the floor. Her shoulder hurt.

As Rose tried to get up there was a huge crash from an upper floor that shook the whole building.

'Wuff!'

The dog gave one small urgent bark and looked at the door. A chunk of ceiling crashed down on to the stairs and the grandfather clock toppled to the ground like a felled tree, hitting the ground with a sickening sound of breaking glass and splintering wood.

Rose struggled painfully to her feet and limped towards the door, stumbling against the wall, the dog trotting beside her, watching her every move. A framed photograph of the Cloth Hall fell to the floor with another crash. Just a few more steps. She could make it. She *had* to make it.

At last. Rose tumbled through the door, and fell straight into someone's arms. She felt the rough khaki on her cheek and knew who it was before he said anything.

'You all right, angel?'

There was a deep roar behind her as the staircase went up in flames. They'd got out just in time.

'I've been looking for you,' said Joe. 'Looking and looking and looking. Ever since – when was it? Night before my birthday, that's right, after me and the boys left the estaminet. I never saw you again.'

'I'm sorry,' Rose said. 'I couldn't help it.'

'And then today, the raid started and I was scared,' he continued. 'They always aim for the clock tower, see, use it as a landmark, and seeing as this place is so close and it was where I first saw you—'

His eyes were level with hers.

'I thought you was inside, Rose.'

'I was,' she said and looked down at the dog. 'He got me out.'

Joe bent down and ruffled the dog's head. 'Our pal, eh? Always there when you're needed, ain't you? You're a good pup.'

Rose looked up at the hotel. The window she'd looked out of that night when she'd heard the soldiers singing in the square was no longer there. The whole of the top of the building had gone, blown off by the shell. Flames leapt up against the sky. She suddenly became very conscious that she was still in Joe's arms. He touched her face with one finger.

'They don't believe in you, Rose. Fred and Tonk.'

'No?'

'Think you're a figment, don't they? That I dreamt you up, gone doolally before I've even seen any action. But I don't care. I know you're real.'

Rose pulled away. 'I've got something of yours.' She drew it out of her coat pocket by its leather thong.

'Mum's lucky sixpence! After all these weeks.'

Weeks? Had it been *weeks* since Rose last saw him? How did that work? She felt a sense of panic rising in her throat. So she was just slipping in and out of random bits of the past? Out of *someone else's* past?

'Rose, you are a miracle.' Joe put the sixpence away in

the pocket of his tunic, the one over his heart. And Rose realised that it wasn't random bits of the past at all. It was Joe's past, and now she was a part of it. So it would be her past too.

He grinned. 'I'll need all the luck I can get where I'm heading.'

Rose felt a clunk in her chest. 'What? Joe . . . You don't mean—'

'Yup! We've got our marching orders. We're off to the Front. In fact' – he watched as some soldiers emerged from a ruined building nearby – 'I need to get back to barracks smartish. We're leaving tonight.'

At first Rose thought he was pretending not to be scared. And then she realised that he really wasn't.

'Tonight? Oh, Joe.'

'It's what we joined up for, Rose. See some action at last, have a pop at Fritz. Tell you what, you can walk along with me, if you want. Show Fred and Tonk that you do exist. If you've got the time, that is,' he added, looking at her from the corner of his eye.

Rose nodded. She had time – she just didn't know how much.

They set off, making their way between the military vehicles and the requisitioned London buses, the dog trotting behind them. As they crossed the square, more people were emerging from their hiding places, looking up at the sky as if they expected something else to fall out of it, and talking excitedly together as people do who've all survived to see another day.

'This way.' Joe indicated a side street with a nod of his head. 'It's a bit rough-going, Rose. Better take care.'

He held out his hand. Rose took it and together they

picked their way over the piles of rubble in the shattered street. You could still see the traces of the homes that had once been there: a smashed-up piano, its sheet music blown about in the wind, an iron bedstead, a single shoe, a patch of flowery wallpaper clinging to a wall.

'Hey, Rose. Look at this.'

Joe had stopped to examine something. It was a stuffed owl, a little brown one, mounted on a branch in the remains of a broken glass case. If Rose had been a bit younger she would have felt sorry for it and wanted to take it home.

'I love owls,' she said, thinking of the green ones all over her pyjamas.

'Me too,' said Joe. 'Lovely silly-looking things. Always surprised by everything, ain't they?'

'It seems a shame to leave him there.'

'Yeah, I know. But what's to be done? Come on, chum.' Joe looked at the dog who was sniffing at the owl. 'You can't eat that. It's just feathers and sawdust.'

They walked on, leaving the owl staring in eternal surprise up at the blue spring sky.

'Here we are, Rose, this is it. Home sweet home.'

It was a muddy square, enclosed on three sides by long low buildings. Steps went up to a sort of open walkway on the first floor where soldiers were leaning against the railings, smoking and chatting.

'Over here, mate! Sid!'

'Oi! Fred!'

A football game was going on, the players in their shirtsleeves, jackets used as improvised goal posts. Just like the boys at school, thought Rose, playing football in the playground.

A shout went up as she and Joe approached.

'Look who it is! The wanderer returns!'

Fred lobbed the ball over towards them. Joe stopped it neatly, then flicked it in the air with his foot before blasting it through the goal to cheers and laughter.

'Where you been, Joe? Off with that imaginary girl of yours?'

There was more laughter at this. Joe grinned at Rose, looking forward to proving them wrong.

'Imaginary? Don't make me laugh, boys—'

'Look at this!' shouted Tonk. 'Joe's brought us a visitor!'

All interest in teasing Joe about his non-existent girl-friend was forgotten as Tonk, Fred and the others crowded round the dog.

'He's a nice little bloke!'

'No collar, mind.'

'His people must've left with the last lot of refugees. Had to leave him behind, poor old mate.'

'We'll adopt him! He can be our mascot.'

'What's his name, Joe?'

Joe looked confused. Rose could see he didn't under-stand why they were ignoring her.

'What? I don't know, chum. Don't think he's got one. He just followed us—'

'Tommy!' shouted Fred.

Everyone laughed, and the dog pricked up his ears as if he recognised the name.

'Tommy. Fine name for him. What do you reckon, mate?'

Tonk addressed this last question to the dog, who wagged his tail politely then looked enquiringly at Joe as if to say, *Is this all right? Do we trust these people?*

Joe squatted down and ruffled the dog's head. 'Don't

you worry, Tommy mate,' he said. 'You're among friends. This is Tonk. He's the stupid one. And that one with the big ears and the daft face is Fred.'

He looked up at Rose.

'And this—' he began, looking round at the grinning faces of his friends, 'this is—'

He was interrupted by the violent ringing of a bell.

'Time to go, chums,' said Fred. 'Let's get loaded up.'

As they started towards the door into the barracks Tonk looked back. 'Joe?'

'I'm with you, mate,' he said. 'Right behind you.'

When they'd gone Joe turned to Rose. His face was puzzled. 'They can't see you, can they, Rose?'

Rose shook her head. 'No one can. Except you – and Tommy.' Tommy wagged his tail at the sound of his name. 'And children,' she added. 'Some children anyway. They can see me.'

Joe took a deep breath. 'Who are you, Rose? What are you doing here?'

Rose shrugged. The sun was lower in the sky now and she was beginning to feel chilly. 'I don't know, Joe. I'm just – a girl.'

'You're not just an anything, Rose. You're an angel.' Then he said, 'My mum did send you, didn't she? To look after me. My own Rose in no-man's-land.'

'Don't be silly.' Rose was embarrassed.

'It's true! I knew you was special when I first spied you looking down at me from the sky the night we arrived. It was the night before my birthday, wasn't it? And you was going to give me a birthday kiss.'

He looked at her, the smile fading from his face. Rose could see herself reflected in his eyes. Although she was conscious of the distant boom of the guns at the Front, in that moment they seemed a long way away. She put a hand up to touch his cheek.

'Joe!'

The moment was gone. Joe turned to the voice, impatient.

'I'm with you, Fred! I'm with you.' He turned back to Rose. She felt very small, standing there in her borrowed coat. 'I've got to go, Rose.'

'I know.'

'I'll see you again, though. I know it.'

'Have you got your lucky sixpence?'

He pulled it out of his pocket. 'Course I have. I don't need it, though. Not now I've got you.'

He gave his funny little salute and headed off towards the barracks. Rose looked down at Tommy, who was looking up at her as if waiting to be told what to do. She crouched down beside him.

'Go with him, Tommy,' she whispered. 'Look after him.'

Tommy didn't hesitate. He trotted after Joe into the barracks, his claws clicking on the cobblestones. Rose waited until she heard the shouts of welcome as the soldiers greeted their new mascot, then she turned and started back to the city.

Perhaps if she kept walking she wouldn't start to cry.

The sun was very low in the sky by the time Rose got back to the square. She sat down with her back against the last remaining wall of the clock tower and watched the activity around her. The procession of refugees had petered out but there was still a lot of movement: troops milling around, women and children being helped on to the backs of lorries, horses huffing and stamping. For the first time since it all began, Rose realised how tired she was. She closed her eyes.

A child's voice was saying something, asking a question in Flemish. Rose opened her eyes. A little girl was looking down at her, a little girl with a green hair ribbon, her grubby face flat and curious – and *familiar*. It was the child from the café . Rose felt ridiculously pleased to see her.

'I don't understand,' she said. She didn't want to frighten her again. 'I'm sorry. I'm English.'

The little girl shrugged and said something else in her rapid, guttural language, then held out her hand. She'd obviously decided this strange-looking person wasn't so terrifying after all. Rose took her hand and allowed the child to pull her to her feet and lead her to where a crowd of women and children were being helped on to the back of a military truck by the Scottish soldiers Rose had seen earlier.

The child's mother spotted her daughter and grabbed her other hand, the one that wasn't clutching Rose's. The truck was nearly full.

'Let's be having you now, ladies, we need to get you out of here before the fun starts.'

A soldier helped the little girl's mother on to the back of the truck and then lifted the child herself, pretending she was a huge weight.

'Whoa! What's your mammy been feeding you on, hen?'

The little girl laughed happily, even though she didn't understand what the soldier had said. When he put her down in the back of the truck she held out her hand to Rose who took it and allowed herself to be pulled up after her. She flopped down on the floor, the little girl's hand small and sticky in her own. The engine started and the truck began to move, bumping and swaying over the broken cobbles, the setting sun shining red through the opening at the back.

No one said a word. Even the babies were silent. The little girl glanced anxiously at her mother, but she was staring straight ahead, her face set and expressionless. Rose squeezed her hand and the child looked up gratefully, before settling down and putting her head on her shoulder. As the truck drove on, leaving the shattered city behind, Rose closed her eyes. And slept.

11

Rose woke with a jerk. For a second she didn't know where she was. Her shoulder hurt and she was so hot her pyjamas were sticking to her skin underneath her coat. As her eyes adjusted to the light she realised she was still in the back of the truck. It was empty now and Rose was alone in the dim green light of the interior with the sun beating down on the canvas roof, the smell reminding her of camping holidays. She wondered where everyone else had gone and missed the comforting feel of the girl's small sticky hand in hers and the weight of her head on her shoulder.

Someone slammed the driver's door at the front, making the vehicle shake, and a male voice shouted, 'This is it, chum. Essex Farm.'

Essex Farm?

Another voice replied to the first, but Rose had stopped listening. She was back at Essex Farm? The cemetery? Had she come back? Back to Grandad and the trip to

Ypres to see Uncle George's grave and the old Rose who was avoiding a Valentine's Day party and sending texts to her dead dad?

The realisation hit Rose with a thud. She hadn't thought about Dad for ages, not since all this had started, whatever it was. She couldn't have *texted* him if she'd wanted to, of course. Her phone was back beside her bed in the hotel in Ypres. In 2014.

But the thing was, she hadn't *wanted* to text him. She hadn't thought about it. What had happened then, had happened then, she realised. A year ago, when Dad died. What was happening now, was happening now. And for the first time, *now* seemed more important than *then*.

But was it still happening now, Rose wondered. Was she still in Joe's world? There was only one way to find out.

She got up. Her shoulder still hurt from when the shell had hit the hotel in Ypres, and she ached all over from lying on the floor of the truck. She half crawled, half staggered to the back and looked through the opening in the canvas.

It was a beautiful day. The sun shone hot on her face, and high in the sky was a single bird, singing its heart out. Rose slid down from the truck and turned her face to the sky. The bird was only just visible, a tiny speck against the blue, and its song soared above another noise, a backdrop of sound that Rose knew she would never forget.

She couldn't work out what it was at first, this relentless grinding roar, a constant thudding and rumbling, like the workings of a giant angry machine. And then she realised: it was the guns, the heavy artillery. And it sounded close. She must be very near the front line.

There were a few other vehicles parked nearby: another military truck, a motorbike and an ambulance. And a truck like the one she'd seen in Ypres when she was trying to talk to Fred and Tonk. Perhaps it was the same one, with its load of wooden crosses.

She could tell that this was the same place, the cemetery she'd visited with Grandad, where she'd put her little bunch of celandines on Joe's grave and where this, this – *thing*, whatever it was, had all started. It was Essex Farm. But it was different.

There were no trees, that was the first thing. The cemetery she'd visited with Grandad had been bounded on three sides by massive trees. This space had no edges. It was just part of the battle-scarred landscape of churned-up earth that stretched out around it. And there were no tidy rows of tombstones standing up from velvet lawns like nicely cleaned teeth. There were just a few tatty wooden crosses, stuck crookedly among the ragged grass, and mounds of earth marking fresh graves.

But there were poppies. Just like everybody always said. Everywhere, there were poppies. Nodding in the long grass between the crosses, papery and delicate and beautiful.

Rose picked one and put her nose in it, recoiling from its bitter smell. Its petals were like silk. She dropped it on the path, where it lay like a clot of blood.

A short distance away some soldiers in shirtsleeves were digging a new grave. They worked silently, throwing the earth into a pile and wiping the sweat off their foreheads with their sleeves. High in the sky the bird, invisible now, was still singing and Rose could still hear the distant grinding rhythm of the guns but, like the remote roar of traffic from a motorway when you're on a country walk, it didn't seem as real as the bird and the sun and the poppies and the men sweating as they dug their comrade's grave.

Rose hated the poppies. They had no right to look so lovely in such an awful place.

The sound of wheels on gravel announced the arrival of another vehicle. Another ambulance. Rose watched, a ghost in the sunshine, as the driver got out, slamming his door, and went round the back where he pulled aside the canvas and – Tommy jumped out.

Her Tommy. Joe's Tommy.

And if Tommy was here . . .?

'What've we got, Corporal?'

The voice wasn't English or Scots. It sounded American – Canadian maybe, Rose couldn't tell the difference – and it belonged to an older soldier with a kind, tired face and a Red Cross armband over his shirt. He reminded Rose of Mr Lee, her favourite teacher at school.

'More gas casualties, sir,' the man replied. 'This is the last of them.'

Gas? Rose's heart clenched with fear. Had Joe been gassed? What did that mean?

She felt something nudge against her leg. It was Tommy. She crouched down with him and watched as the driver and the medical officer helped the injured men out of the back of the ambulance. Everything seemed to be happening in slow motion. The men's eyes were streaming and they staggered against each other, coughing and retching and fighting for breath. Rose saw that the brass buttons of their uniforms had turned bright green.

She searched each face that passed as the men made their painful way towards the bunkers of the dressing station. The first three were black soldiers, North African troops in the blue-grey uniforms of the French army. The next was a Scotsman in his khaki kilt. And then . . .

'Joe!'

He looked terribly small next to the others, and quite different from the funny, fearless boy Rose had last seen in Ypres. How long ago was that? It felt like centuries. He was hunched and shrunken with pain. She didn't think she could bear it. But she had to.

'JOE!'

He looked around vaguely at the sound of Rose's voice, unable to see much through his poor streaming eyes. Then Tommy gave a little bark and Joe's face softened into a smile as his eyes rested on them crouched together in the sun.

'Rose . . .' Her name came out in a croak and ended in a fit of terrible wrenching coughs.

The driver took his arm and led him after the others. 'Come on, chum. This way. You're safe now.'

Rose had seen the row of small, cave-like rooms of the dressing station when she'd visited this place with Grandad, but then they were made of concrete. Now they were built of wood which made them look insecure and temporary. On the step of the first bunker a couple of medical orderlies with their Red Cross armbands were sitting smoking in the sunshine. Behind them, Rose could just make out another man asleep on a bunk. Outside the second bunker, Tommy stopped, looking up at her.

'This one?' she said. 'You'd better wait outside.'

Tommy sat down and watched as Rose stepped in, slipping into the gloom like a shadow. The officer, the one with the accent, shot a quick puzzled look in her direction before turning back to the hunched figure on the bench.

'What's your name, son?'

'Joe. Sir.'

Each word was wrung out with a terrible effort. Rose could hear Joe struggling to breathe, the air rattling horribly in his chest.

'Rifleman. Valentine. Joe. Strud—' The word was swallowed in a fit of coughing.

'It's all right, son. Don't talk any more. We'll do what we can to make you more comfortable.'

Rose slipped over and knelt down beside Joe's bench, brushing past the officer as she went. He drew his breath and gave another sharp look in her direction, before turning away. Joe's head was thrown back, tears streaming from his tightly closed eyes. She took his hand. It felt dry and rough and cold. He opened his bloodshot eyes and looked at her with a trace of his old grin. He took a juddering breath as he prepared to speak. Then:

'Sorry. Rose. Got to be. Sick.'

He turned his face and threw up in a well-placed bucket on the floor. Rose kept hold of his hand until it was over. He took a deep breath and wiped his mouth on his sleeve. His breath didn't sound so painful now.

'Feel a bit better after that, Joe?' said the officer.

'Yes. Sir. Thank. You. Sir.'

'How old are you, son?'

'Nineteen. Sir.'

There was a trace of defiance in his voice. He was feeling better, Rose thought.

The officer sighed. 'I'm not a fool, son.'

Joe said nothing. Rose squeezed his hand as the officer lifted Joe's other one and took his pulse, nodding his head as if pleased.

'Listen, Private Strudwick,' he said. 'Joe. This is what's going to happen. I'm sending you back to Blighty.'

Rose's heart leapt.

'Thank you. Sir.'

'You're going to be poorly for a long time,' the officer continued. 'But I've seen worse. With the right care, you should pull through. You're lucky to be alive, you know.'

'Yes. Sir.'

'So let's keep it that way, shall we? When you get better, which I think you will, and they send you home from hospital, I want you to go to your father and tell him to write to the War Office. Tell them you lied about your age when you joined up. If he sends them your birth certificate they'll have no choice but to discharge you from the army.'

Rose thought the medical officer had the kindest face in the world. She squeezed Joe's hand again. Was it possible? Was he really going to be all right?

'I can't. Do that. Sir.'

What?

'Come on, son. You're not the only boy who lied about his age to join up.'

'Sorry, sir. No. Sir. I must. Come back.'

What?!

'How old are you, son? Really?'

'Old enough. To fight.'

Rose felt herself getting angry. She was glad the officer was so calm.

'Tell me the truth now, Private,' he said. 'What are you? Seventeen? Sixteen?'

Rose glared at Joe: *Tell him the truth.*

He looked at her out of the corner of his eye and grinned faintly. 'Fifteen. Sir.'

The officer closed his eyes for a second and drew a long

shuddering breath. 'Someone should be shot for this,' he said, almost to himself. 'And it's not those poor bastards across the canal.'

'It's not for. Me. Sir. It's my two. Best. Pals. They've—' The officer looked at him sharply as he fought for breath. 'Gone. Sir.'

Not both of them? Fred and Tonk? Tonk and Fred? Oh, Joe. Not both *of them . . .*

'I'm sorry to hear that, Private.'

Rose thought of the last time she saw them back at the barracks, kicking a ball about in the sunshine, like boys from her school. What was it Joe had said?

Tonk, he's the stupid one. And that one with the big ears and the daft face is Fred . . .

'Got to fight. On. Sir. For. Their sake. Else—' Joe doubled up in a fit of coughing, then managed to get out his last words. '—What's. The. Point?'

The officer shook his head and turned away so Rose couldn't see his face.

There was a voice from the sunlit doorway: 'More casualties coming in, sir.'

The officer sighed. 'Thank you, Corporal.' He turned back to Joe. 'I can't make you do anything, Joe,' he said, 'but I hope you'll reconsider. This war is terrible enough. We don't need to sacrifice boys.'

He moved to the doorway, suddenly seeming very old and weary. Joe looked at Rose and grinned, then coughed and called after the officer as well as he could:

'Who. Are you calling. A boy. Sir?'

But the officer had gone. Rose drew a deep breath. Beneath the sharp hospital smell of disinfectant in the bunker was a darker stench of damp and despair.

'I'm sorry about your friends, Joe.'

Joe looked at her, his eyes streaming. Was it the effect of the gas or tears for his friends?

'You. Understand. Don't you, Rose? Why—' He doubled up with coughs again.

'I think so.' He squeezed her hand. 'But it won't bring them back, Joe. It won't help them if you die too.'

'I won't. Die. Rose.' He stopped and fought for breath, then continued. 'I've got me lucky. Sixpence. And Tommy. And. You.'

Rose thought for a minute. A lot depended on what she was going to say next, and she wanted to get it right.

'My dad died last year, Joe.' The words came out quickly now. 'And ever since then I've done nothing. Not really. I've done nothing except think about him and dream about him and wish I was back in the past with him. It's like I've been in a sort of bubble, avoiding people, avoiding the real world.'

Rose hadn't thought about it before, but that was what it had been like. She was glad she'd realised it.

'What. About. Your mum?'

'She's been in a bubble too,' said Rose. 'And I've been no help. She just makes me think how much I miss him. So I can't look at her, or talk to her, not really. I've made it worse.'

'Poor. Lady.'

'Yeah.' Rose took a deep breath. Thoughts and feelings were buzzing around in her head, jostling for position. They'd been there for a long time, but it was only now that she was able to sort them out. To listen to them.

'What I mean,' she said, her thoughts becoming clearer as she spoke, 'or what I think I mean . . .'

She paused. Joe's eyes were fixed on her face. He gave a tiny nod as if to tell her to carry on.

'... is that Dad wouldn't want me to be like this.'

He nodded again. She went on, still choosing her words carefully.

'Whatever I do, however sad I feel, it's not going to bring him back. He'd want me to live. And I think Fred and Tonk would want you to live too.'

Joe took a deep rattling breath. 'I will. Live. Rose. I—'

He broke down in a fit of coughing. Rose finished the sentence for him.

'Promise?'

Before he could reply, one of the stretcher-bearers stuck his head through the doorway. 'Private Strudwick? Time to go, chum.'

Joe looked around as he tried to struggle to his feet. 'Tom?' he said. 'Tom-my?'

'That's right, mate. We're all Tommies here. You're among friends now.'

'He means his dog, Bert,' said another voice. 'Little pup that was with him in the trenches.'

'Oh, yeah. Don't you worry about Tommy, chum. We'll look after him. He's sitting outside in the sun right now watching the dicky birds.'

'I'll make sure he's all right, Joe,' said Rose.

Joe turned and smiled at her. You could warm your hands on that smile.

'You all right to walk, mate?' The stretcher-bearer helped Joe to his feet and Rose released his hand.

'Joe—'

'Don't. Worry. Rose. I'll be all. Right.'

'But—'

He said it again: 'I've got me lucky. Sixpence. Ain't I? And Tommy. And. You.'

For a moment his silhouette was dark against the sunlit doorway. Then he was gone.

12

Rose took a deep breath and stepped out of the greenish gloom of the bunker. The sun was still beating down and the poppies were nodding their scarlet heads along to the rhythm of the guns.

Joe's going to be all right, she thought. *He promised.*

Tommy was sitting on the grass, watching the injured men as they struggled into the back of the ambulance. Rose was glad to see that someone had given him a bowl of water.

The mood among the injured men had changed. They were going home, back to Blighty! In spite of their pain and the terrible laboured wheezing in their chests, they were managing to crack jokes, slapping each other on the back. One of them even tried to sing – *'Take me back to dear old Blighty . . .'* – before he was convulsed by a coughing fit, amidst friendly jeers from the others that ended up with them choking and fighting for breath as well.

Joe was the last in line. Rose's heart lifted as he turned and gave her a tiny wave before the medical orderlies helped him into the vehicle. He was going home, he really was. He was going to be safe after all.

And then a soldier walked past, obstructing her view of the ambulance for a second. He was heading towards the cemetery. He had a spade over his shoulder and his face was pale in spite of the hot day.

The driver slammed the door of his cab and started the engine. And as Rose watched the soldier walking across the cemetery, past the spot where she'd seen Joe's grave, she realised something: the cemetery was only half full.

Not even that, actually. There was only a handful of graves compared to the hundreds she'd seen when she was there with Grandad. The ground with its long grass and its beautiful nodding poppies was just lying there, waiting. Waiting to swallow up more young men.

And one of them was going to be Joe. She'd seen his grave: *V.J. Strudwick*, it said, and the date he'd been killed: 14 January 1916. Exactly one month before his sixteenth birthday.

And that was when the truth hit her. She hadn't convinced him. Joe was still planning to come back. To fight on behalf of his friends. To die in France on a cold January day.

Unless . . . Could she warn him, tell him what was going to happen – that if he came back he would be killed? Tell him he must stay in England, like the officer said, admit he'd lied about his age, get himself discharged from the army, go back to his mum, to school, to whatever he was doing before this all started.

To live.

Was it possible to change the past?

The driver had finally got his engine to fire up and the ambulance was pulling away, out into the lane.

'Wait!'

Tommy looked up, startled, as Rose tore after the vehicle, hair and coat flying, stumbling over the rutted ground.

'WAIT!'

No one could hear her, of course. And only Tommy could see her, in her borrowed coat, watching the ambulance disappear down the road. But then she heard something else: a motorbike was being kicked into life.

Tommy barked. Rose whirled round. The rider was astride his bike, goggles over his eyes, cap held on by a strap under his chin. Was he following the ambulance? Rose had no way of knowing – he might be heading for the front line – but she had to take the risk.

As the rider kicked the bike's starter again, Rose jumped. She flung one pyjama-clad leg over the seat and grabbed him around the waist. The rider shuddered as if he'd felt a sudden breath of icy air on his back, but then shook himself, revved the bike's engine and zoomed off in a shower of gravel.

They were off.

Rose hid her face in his jacket and clung on, the engine making her body vibrate and her teeth chatter. She could just hear Tommy barking as the bike swerved out on to the lane and she felt the wind in her hair and the roughness of the rider's jacket beneath her cheek. She could smell oil and petrol and the now familiar scent of the British Tommy: tobacco and sweat, unwashed woollen uniform and the faintest whiff of peppermint.

Rose had never been on a motorbike before, even as a passenger. And she was scared at first, too scared to open her eyes or raise her face from where it was hidden in the back of the rider's jacket. She hung on to him with all her strength, her arms clamped so tightly around his waist that it should've stopped him breathing, her teeth clenched in fear and determination.

I am not afraid, not afraid, not afraid . . .

And after a while she wasn't. She actually started to enjoy the feel of the wind in her hair and the tilt of the bike as the rider manoeuvred it around bends in the road. She opened one eye, just one, keeping her cheek firmly against the rider's jacket, and watched the fields whizz by in a blur of green and gold and red. They were heading away from the front line, and the countryside didn't look very different from the landscape she and Grandad had passed through on the train. There were the same flat fields, lines of trees pointing up at the sky, neat farmhouses with cows and horses outside. Rose even saw a woman hanging out her washing as they shot past. It seemed strange that normal life with washing and cooking and growing vegetables, was going on so close to the battlefields where soldiers were dying.

After a while, Rose felt even braver and raised her head from the rider's back so she could look beyond him to the road ahead. Would she see the ambulance? The wind was making her eyes water, but yes – there it was, easily visible in the flat countryside. So she still had a chance, she told herself. To find Joe, tell him to stay in England. Make sure he didn't come back.

The fields soon started to give way to rows of little brick houses and it became clear they were entering a town, smaller and less important than Ypres, but still thronged with troops. Everywhere Rose looked there were men in khaki, sitting outside café s, hanging about on corners, chatting and smoking and laughing. Why were they all here? She guessed they must be on leave; they came to this little town when they had a few days off from the Front. But where was Joe being taken? And would her motorcyclist take her to the same place?

While Rose was thinking, he pulled up and parked the bike next to some other military vehicles. Then he dismounted, slithering free of Rose's ghostly clutches as if she wasn't there, and ran up the steps of a building that looked like a smaller version of the Cloth Hall in Ypres.

Rose sat for a moment, balanced uncomfortably on the back of the bike. Now that the engine had stopped, she realised she could barely hear the thud of the guns from the Front. It was just a dull background heartbeat behind all the normal sounds of humanity. Men laughing and talking, children shrieking and being scolded by their mothers. The clink of glasses and clatter of plates from the café s, hoofbeats on cobbles and trucks driving by. Life seemed ordinary here. Apart from all the troops, it was almost as if the war didn't exist.

But where was Joe?

As Rose clambered off the bike, wondering what to do, an ambulance drove past. It wasn't as big as the one that had been carrying Joe and the other soldiers from Essex Farm, but she guessed it might be going to the same place. She ran after it, slipping through the crowds, away from the square and into a busy side street. The ambulance disappeared around a corner, but she kept on running, running, running. She had to find Joe.

Her chest was burning and she was dripping with sweat inside her heavy borrowed coat when she finally saw a group of military ambulances, parked outside what looked like a small railway station. And, yes, there were wounded men being helped out of them – some on stretchers, some walking – guided by businesslike young women in nurses' uniforms: long skirts with white aprons, red crosses on the linen caps that covered their hair. Most of them looked young, some not much not older than Rose. She squeezed in amongst them, staring into the faces of the wounded men. Each one of them had a home to go to and a story to tell. But none of them was Joe.

Rose hurried on, weaving through the crowd, heading towards the station. The wounded men must be going on a train. A train that would take them to the coast, where a boat would take them back to England. And if Joe was with them she had to find him. Because once he was back in England she might never see him again. And then how would she tell him that he mustn't come back?

By the time Rose pushed her way through the station, sweat was dripping into her eyes, but she wasn't going to stop even for the seconds it would take to remove her coat. There was no time. The platform was even more packed with men in khaki, both fit and wounded. Some looked as if they'd just arrived. Their uniforms were clean and neat and they were hiding their anxiety with jokes and banter. Others were filthy and silent, their faces taut and closed. They were going home on leave, Rose guessed, or at least somewhere away from the fighting, but they didn't look relieved or excited. They just looked blank and exhausted as if they'd never be capable of feeling anything again. The nurses buzzed around the wounded men, supporting the ones on crutches, tending to the ones on stretchers. Rose noticed that the new arrivals avoided looking at the wounded men with their grey, resigned faces and their bloody bandages.

Again she went in amongst them, slipping through the crowds like a fish, looking at faces, searching for her Joe. An older nurse with a crucifix around her neck crossed herself and muttered a prayer as she passed, but Rose didn't care. She had a job to do.

She was beginning to lose hope when there was a ripple through the waiting crowd and a small cheer went up from some of the men. A train was approaching. The nurses started to busy themselves with their patients, helping those who could walk to the edge of the platform, lifting the stretchers of those who were helpless.

'Good luck, chum!'

'See you back in Blighty!'

'Not if I see you first!'

There were grins and backslaps. But there was no sign of Joe.

The train drew up at the platform with a sigh of steam and a hiss of brakes. Doors were flung open and people surged towards it. Rose could see that the train had been specially adapted to transport the injured men. Some carriages had seats, others were lined with bunks, three deep on either side. It was a sort of hospital on wheels.

The stretcher-bearers delivered their burdens, nurses guided their patients, doors were slammed, the platform was emptying . . .

And still there was no sign of Joe.

Then, as the last door was slammed and the guard raised his whistle to his lips, there was a cry from the far end of the platform.

'Wait!'

It was a young nurse with a pale, determined face, leading a small group of men. Men who were staggering and coughing and half blind. They were the gas casualties from Essex Farm.

'Joe!'

He looked around at the sound of her voice, but he couldn't see her. His eyes were too bad and the platform was too crowded. A big soldier on crutches stepped in front of Rose and by the time she'd managed to slip past him, the young nurse and her patients were on the train and the door was slammed behind them.

Joe had gone.

Rose didn't stop to think. A wounded Tommy with a bandaged head was leaning out of the window of the door nearest to her, accepting a last cigarette from his mate.

The guard blew his whistle.

The train gathered its energy in a great huff of steam.

And Rose jumped, catching the top of the open window with both hands just as the train started to heave itself away from the platform. She hung on as the bandaged Tommy shouted his last goodbyes:

'See you, boys! Be lucky!'

As the train began to gather speed, Rose used all her strength to drag herself up. First she got one elbow on the edge of the open window, then the other. She was now so close to the soldier that she could smell the disinfectant of his bandage and the tobacco on his breath. As she hoisted her body up, he flinched and moved away, back into the carriage.

Rose was halfway through now. Her head was inside the

train, while her legs were waving about outside, and the edge of the window was digging painfully into her stomach. One more heave and she was inside, in a heap on the floor. She was bruised and filthy and exhausted. But she'd done it. She was on the train.

She struggled to her feet and looked around. The carriage was lined with seats, facing a central aisle, each one taken by a wounded soldier. Some seemed to be gas casualties, but none was Joe.

'Nurse!'

The cries of the wounded men followed Rose as she made her way along the train. Were they talking to her?

'Nurse!'

She'd got on near the front, in the carriage next to the engine, so she knew that if she walked back through the train, she'd be sure to find him.

'Nurse!'

The young women looked crisp and clean and calm, with their spotless uniforms and gentle efficiency. No wonder the men called them angels. Joe had called her an angel on that snowy night back in Ypres. His angel in the snow. It seemed a lifetime away.

'Nurse!'

The cries became part of the rhythm of the train as it ground its way through the countryside, great clouds of white steam rolling past the windows.

'Nurse!'

Rose stumbled on through another carriage, this one lined with bunks. The men were quieter here, lying with their eyes closed or staring into the thick grey light that filtered through the window blinds. Surely the light hadn't been so dim when the train left?

As Rose passed through the carriage, swaying with the movement of the train, something touched her hand. She turned and met the blue-grey eyes of a young man lying on one of the bunks.

'Nurse?' he said. His voice was very weak.

Did he mean her? Rose looked around. There was no nurse to be seen, so she turned back to him. And he smiled. It was one of the happiest smiles she'd ever seen. And there was no doubt about it – he was smiling at her.

'Nurse.' He said it as if to confirm her existence.

'I'm sorry,' Rose was flustered, 'I'm not a nurse actually. I can't—'

The young man smiled again. 'No,' he said. 'I know what you are.'

He held out his hand. Rose took it. It was rough and dry and very cold.

'Warm,' said the young man. His voice wasn't much more than a whisper now. 'I didn't expect you to feel – warm.'

'You're going to be all right,' said Rose.

It was what her mum used to say when she was ill or upset. And it always made Rose feel better, even when she knew it wasn't true. It wasn't true now, she was pretty sure of that. The young soldier wasn't going to be all right. That was why he could see her.

Rose felt quite calm now. She smiled down at him and repeated her lie: 'You're going to be all right.'

The young man squeezed her hand and smiled a sleepy smile. 'I'm all right now,' he murmured. 'Lying here. Holding your hand. This. Is. Heaven.'

Rose didn't know what to say. She brushed strands of fair hair back from his cold damp forehead and smiled into his eyes.

'Thank. You,' he whispered. He drew a long, shuddering breath then turned his head away. The smile froze on his face, as if he'd turned into a photograph of himself.

Rose gently detached her hand and moved away as a young nurse hurried up to her patient. There was nothing anybody could do for him now. And she had to find Joe.

'Nurse!'

When had a train ever been so long? Rose's legs felt heavy, and her eyes had dimmed. The outlines of the bunks and the nurses and the hands that reached out to grab her coat as she passed were just shadows in the thick, grey mist that seemed to be filling the carriages.

'Nurse!'

The voices of the men and the whispers of the nurses were getting fainter and fainter like the memory of something that had happened a long time ago.

'Nurse!'

Like the smell of her dad's jumper after he'd been working on the allotment. Or the smile on his face when he came to pick her up from school. It was all drifting out of reach.

Except for Joe.

He was the only thing that mattered. There was nothing now but the rhythm of the wheels and the grinding of her thoughts as the train hurtled on.

She had to find him. She had to find him. She had to find him . . .

And then, just as she thought she couldn't go any further, a terrible scream sliced through the air (was it the train's whistle? The screech of its brakes? *Was it her?*), then an almighty crash and a horrible, shuddering hiss as the train crunched to a halt.

And Rose fell. Down, down, down.

She wasn't conscious of hitting the floor. She wasn't conscious of anything at all.

13

When Rose opened her eyes she saw nothing. There was no difference between the darkness behind her closed eyelids and the darkness around her. For one awful moment she thought she'd gone blind, and then she looked up and realised she could see a few stars twinkling in the black. So it was night-time and she was outside. There was no sound.

And it was terribly, terribly cold.

Her borrowed coat was long and heavy and thick, but all she had underneath it were her owl pyjamas, and they weren't enough. No socks, no vest, no scarf, no gloves. Her feet were freezing inside her boots and her hands ached. It was the sort of cold when you couldn't imagine ever being warm again.

Then there was the smell.

It was like nothing she'd ever experienced. Like filth and muck and rubbish bins and the time the downstairs loo got blocked and flooded the kitchen and Mum had to get in a man called Dave the Drain who'd stood there in the middle of it in his wellies and poked a stick down the toilet.

This smell was worse than that, actually. There was a horrible sweetness about it that stuck in your throat and clung to the inside of your nose and got into your head and curled itself around your brain like smoke. Rose had the feeling that it would be with her for the rest of her life, following her like a guilty memory.

She reached out her hand in the dark and felt the ground next to where she was half sitting, half lying, her back propped against something. It was icy cold and wet. Sticky.

Rose shuddered and huddled down in her coat, breathing in the faint violet scent of its previous owner. She tried to remember. She'd been on the train – yes, that was it, the hospital train – looking for Joe, when it had stopped suddenly and she'd fallen. She must have hit her head or something, she didn't know. But where was she now?

If only it wasn't so dark. And quiet – the thick black air was heavy with silence. It was like she was alone in the darkness with only that smell for company. And she thought, for the second time since this – whatever-it-was – had started, *Am I dead? Did the train crash? Was it hit by a shell? Did we all die?*

Her thoughts were interrupted by a boom, a sound so faint it was almost gentle, and the world lit up.

It was the whitest, brightest light Rose had ever seen, and for the ten or twenty seconds it lasted, everything was as clear and sharp as a glossy black-and-white photograph. Muddy walls on two sides, wooden boards on the ground, humped shapes sprinkled with snow, piles of rifles, shovels, rubbish, bits of wood, filthy tarpaulins, a dented petrol can, a tin helmet, a dog.

A dog?

There was a rattle of gunfire, and then the light died and the darkness was deeper than ever.

'Tommy?' Rose whispered.

She heard his paws tapping along the wooden boards towards her, then felt a wet nose in her hand.

Tommy! She buried her face in his fur and felt his tail thumping against her legs and she thought, *If Tommy's here . . .*

When she looked up, Rose realised that the darkness wasn't as deep as it had been. It was beginning to look grainy, like slush, and she could make out vague grey shapes. Someone somewhere started to sing:

'Roses are shining in Picardy . . .'

Another voice shouted at him to shut up, and then, to Rose's right, there was a rasping sound as someone struck a match. As the flame flared Rose saw, only a few feet away, the soldier light his cigarette. He was slumped against the muddy wall like she was, so covered in mud and filth that he seemed to be part of it, as if he'd grown out of the earth.

Rose watched him smoking in the thick grey light, his cigarette glowing as he inhaled, and she realised where she was.

She was in a trench. On the front line. And over there, where the bright white light had gone up, was the German army.

The air was getting less solid now, and through the mist Rose could make out more shapes. Next to her was a huddled brownish-grey heap, half covered with a tarpaulin and speckled with snow. Rose put out her hand to touch it, and then withdrew it quickly. There was a pair of boots sticking out from the end, cracked filthy boots encrusted with mud.

It was a man. Asleep or . . .?

The shape stirred and groaned. Asleep. Thank goodness.

Rose heaved herself up with an effort. Her body was sore and shivering, and there was still a sharp pain in her shoulder from where she'd fallen in the hotel. She wrapped her borrowed coat around herself as tightly as she could and looked down at the dog.

Where is he, Tom?

Did he get back to England safely?

Did he recover from the gas?

And then, in spite of what she and the officer had said to him:

Did he come back?

Tommy seemed to understand what she was thinking. He turned and trotted off along the trench, casting a look back as if he expected Rose to follow him. She took a deep breath and stepped over the mud-encrusted legs of the sleeping soldier. Then, as the dark grey of the night started to turn into the light grey of the dawn, she set off along the trench after the dog.

She slipped past another humped shape, slithering on the slippery wooden boards that covered the ground, and turned a corner. There were deep ledges and cubby holes carved out of the walls of the trench, where Rose could make out more sleeping forms. Sometimes she had to step over the legs of men who were propped up against the sides, heads slumped on their chests, their faces hidden.

Another corner and Rose nearly fell over someone. 'Sorry!' she said, automatically, realising she was standing on his hand. Of course, he couldn't hear her. Joe was the only one who could. And Tommy, of course.

But there was another reason.

As Rose moved her foot and looked down at his face in the grainy grey light, she realised with a thud of horror why he would never respond.

This soldier was dead.

There was no mistaking it. He was lying on his back on the muddy boards with his eyes open. There was blood on his tunic, thick and dark in the gloom, but it was his face that left Rose in no doubt.

She'd never seen a dead person before, not one who'd been dead a while. They'd asked her if she wanted to see her dad, but she'd said no. She hadn't really known why, but she could tell Mum was relieved. She'd always thought a dead person might look like they were asleep, much the same as when they were alive, just still and quiet and peaceful.

But she'd be wrong.

There was no way this man could be asleep. His face was so strange and sunken-looking, it was almost as if he'd never been alive. He was just a shell, an object. Rose tried to think of the person he'd once been, of his face laughing or sad or looking into someone else's eyes. But she couldn't. It was like he'd never existed. That was the worst thing.

And then, as she went to step over him, another thought hit her. All those other soldiers, the ones she'd thought were asleep, whose faces she couldn't see – were they dead too?

Rose looked up at the strip of sky above the trench. It was getting lighter. The air was becoming less opaque and the sky had a greenish tint. A new day was about to begin.

'Wuff!'

Rose turned as Tommy gave one of his polite little barks and she saw him. He was there. Lying on his back on one of the muddy shelves cut into the side of the trench, a helmet tilted over his eyes.

Joe. Even though she couldn't see his face, she knew it was him.

Rose dropped down beside him, not caring about the icy slush that soaked through the knees of her pyjamas. Was he dead too? She felt Tommy's body, warm against her side.

Please let him not be dead, please.

Tommy snuffled at her hand.

Please.

She brushed the snow off the tarpaulin that covered Joe.

Please . . .

He smiled. Then, without moving his helmet, he said, 'There you are.'

A shaft of light penetrated the trench and the same voice as before sang: *'There's never a rose like you . . .'*

Rose felt angry. 'You came back!'

Joe tipped the helmet back from his face and sat up, swinging his legs off the shelf and looking down at her with those bright brown eyes. His face was so grey and tired and dirty it was like a mask. But his eyes were the same. He looked like a cheeky wild animal watching her from behind a hedge.

'I had to,' he said.

'You didn't. How could you? After what happened to your friends.'

Joe shook his head. 'That's *why* I had to, Rose.'

'I don't understand.'

'They were my best mates,' he said. 'I couldn't leave

126

them here on their own.'

'But—'

'I had to do something. And this' – he gestured at the desolate scene – 'this was all I could do.'

He's different, thought Rose. *Older. Or maybe just really, really tired.*

'It won't change nothing, I know that,' he was saying. 'None of it will.'

'Then why—?'

'People like us, Rose, we just want to live happy quiet lives, don't we? Little house. Enough to eat. We don't know what this is all about, this *war*.' Joe spat out the word as if it was a piece of bad meat. 'And if we did, we wouldn't care.'

'So why, then? *Why* did you have to come back?'

Joe shrugged. 'Cos I'd rather be dead than spend the rest of me life feeling bad about me mates.'

'It's not your fault they died.'

'I know that.' Joe sounded as if he'd been thinking about this a lot. 'But they did, Rose, and I didn't and I can't bear it.'

Rose felt her eyes fill with tears. 'Oh, Joe,' she whispered. She did understand, of course she did. She felt the same about Dad. 'I just . . . I wanted you to be safe. That's all.' Her voice went up in a squeak as she tried to fight back her tears.

Joe patted the ledge next to him. His movements had lost their old quickness, and he didn't crackle with energy like he used to, but his eyes still twinkled as Rose sat down.

'It's my birthday soon,' he said, with a trace of his old grin. 'A month today.'

'Valentine's Day,' said Rose.

'Yup. I'll be sixteen. What an age, eh?'

He held up one filthy forefinger and touched Rose's face. His expression grew serious as he looked at her. 'I made you something, Rose.'

'A present?'

'Yeah. While I was in the hospital, coughing my guts up into a bucket. I haven't got it here, though, wasn't sure I'd see you. Left it in Wipers.'

Rose was ashamed how disappointed she felt. She really wanted that present. 'I'll never find it there.'

'Ah, but you will,' said Joe. 'That's the cleverness of it. D'you remember the hidey-hole we found last winter? In the wall of the old ramparts?'

Rose remembered. It had been snowing that day too. Was it really almost a year ago?

'It was the night before your birthday,' she said.

'That's right.' He gave her his old look out of the corner of his eyes. 'And you was going to give me a birthday kiss.'

Rose didn't know what to say. She held his gaze as long as she could before looking away.

'Anyway!' Joe was grinning properly now. 'When we heard we was coming out here, I left it there, your present. Right at the back of that hidey-hole where Tommy chased the cat.' Tommy wagged his tail at the mention of his name. 'Yes, you, you rascal!'

'Who looked after him when you were back home?'

'Chaps, I dunno. Everybody loves Tommy, don't they, mate?' The dog wagged his tail again, as if he was glad to have his two favourite people in the same place.

'I told him to look after you,' said Rose.

'And he has done, haven't you, boy?' Joe turned to Rose,

his face serious again. 'Promise me something, Rose.'

'What?'

'That you'll go and find it. Your present. If I don't come back.'

'Come back from what?' Rose felt her voice rising again. His birthday was a month today, that's what he said. So that made today 14 January 1916.

A month before his sixteenth birthday.

It couldn't be. Not today. Not *today.*

'Come back from what?' she repeated. 'What d'you mean? Joe?'

'Wakey wakey!'

'Joe!'

An older soldier was making his way along the trench and everywhere the grey humps were stirring and revealing themselves to be sleeping soldiers.

'Rise and shine, boys,' the old soldier continued. 'The sun is coming up on a brand-new day.'

You'd have thought there'd be complaints and banter from the soldiers at being woken so early, but none of them said a word. They didn't even look at each other as they gathered their kit together and picked up their rifles.

'Stand to!'

The soldiers leapt to attention, all facing the same side of the trench. Joe was with them. Rose saw there were ladders propped against the muddy walls. She was trembling, and it wasn't because of the cold. She got up and touched Joe's sleeve. 'What does it mean? Joe? What's happening?'

She wasn't even sure she'd said it out loud, but Joe flicked a quick look in her direction as another man made his way down the trench. He was in a different uniform from the others, cleaner and smarter. In the midst of her panic Rose guessed he was an officer, even though he didn't look that much older than Joe. An image flashed up in her mind of the boys from the sixth form college where most of the people from her school went on to do A levels. He looked just like them. Behind him another young soldier was carrying a bottle which he offered to the men. They held out tin cups and threw back the liquid he poured out for them. Rose caught its sharp chemical smell.

'Joe?' Her voice was no more than a whisper.

Joe swallowed his drink quickly with a slight shudder. 'This is it, Rose,' he said quietly.

'What?' she said. She decided to carry on feeling angry, because she didn't want to feel anything else. 'What is "it", Joe?'

'We're going over the top. Do you know what that means?'

Rose knew.

A shell flew over, its horrible fluttering whine sounding quite familiar now. There was a half-hearted cheer from the men as it exploded over the German line with a stomach-churning boom.

'One of ours,' Joe murmured. 'Little taster for them. Then it's our turn.'

More shells went over. The earth shuddered with noise. The young officer was studying his watch. He nodded to the older man, the one who'd woken the soldiers.

'FIX!' the old soldier yelled.

There was a swish and a clatter as the men drew blades from their kit. Then waited.

'BAYONETS!'

The men obeyed as one, attaching the blades to the ends of their rifles. They did it automatically, like men in a dream. Another shell flew over towards the German line.

Rose looked up at the strip of whitish-grey sky above the trench. She felt – empty. She hadn't been able to save him. In the end, all this had been for nothing.

The men gazed at the muddy wall of the trench. One soldier crossed himself and whispered a prayer. Another looked at a little photograph in his hand. The rest of them just stood. And waited. The officer stared at his watch. The sky was getting lighter.

'How about that kiss?'

Joe's voice was just a whisper in her ear. Rose turned her face towards him and looked into his eyes, unable to speak.

She wasn't aware of moving towards him but she did. As the sky turned pale in the cold winter dawn and the men stood waiting like statues, Rose closed her eyes and felt Joe's lips on hers, cool and gentle and a bit rough. Another shell exploded, making the earth shudder. It was like the end of the world.

Joe pulled away and looked at Rose, his face still only inches away from hers. He touched her cheek with one finger. 'My Rose in no-man's-land,' he whispered.

'Joe—'

'I've got to do this.'

Why? Rose thought. *It's not fair! I can't lose you too. Not after Dad, not after all this!* But she didn't say that. She said, 'I know.'

'Look after Tommy, won't you?'

'Of course.'

'Promise?'

'I promise.'

He kissed her again. She wanted to cling to him, hold on to him, beg him not to go. But she didn't. She just stood there, trembling, watching his face to make sure she would never forget the smallest detail: the little scar above his eyebrow, the single freckle on the side of his nose. His grin.

'Don't forget your present,' he said.

'I won't.'

He let go of her. 'Bye, Rose. And – thanks.'

But I didn't do anything, said a desperate little voice in her head. Joe seemed to hear it.

'Believe me, love,' he murmured. 'You did.'

The officer drew his pistol with one hand, and with the other held a whistle to his lips. The men tensed, like runners at the start of a race.

'Joe – I can't bear—'

'You can, Rose. Trust me. You can. You will.'

Rose sank to the ground and put her arms round Tommy. The whistle blew, the sound cutting through the air like a scream, and the men started to move up the ladders. Joe gave her his funny little salute, then turned to join his mates.

And the world exploded.

14

Rose was woken by the buzz of her phone. She opened her eyes to sunshine slanting through window blinds. She was lying in her bed in the neat white hotel room with the picture of poppies on the wall.

She was back.

Whatever had happened had happened. And now it was over. She didn't know how she'd got back. Or why. All she knew was that she'd loved someone and lost him. Again.

It wasn't fair.

Rose reached for her phone, grimacing in pain. Her shoulder still hurt from last night, or whenever it was that shell had hit the hotel and nearly killed her. Joe's story had come to an end, she thought, and all she was left with was a bruised shoulder and a broken heart.

The text was from Grandad:

Good morning sleepy head. Have gone for walk. See you 12 outside hotel x

Sleepy head? Rose checked the time. It was nearly ten o'clock. Grandad must have been up for hours.

She swung her legs on to the floor and stared at the tiny specks of dust twinkling in the bands of sunlight, wondering what to do. The bright modern room seemed less real to her than the mud of the trenches.

Did it really happen?

There was no sign of the heavy coat that had kept out the cold of a winter's day a hundred years ago. Rose remembered its faint smell of Parma violets and dust, and wished she'd kept the button she'd felt in the pocket as a souvenir. She would have liked to look at it and try to imagine the face of the coat's owner and think about what might have happened to her. Was it the girl she'd heard singing in her room last night? A girl like her, who'd lost someone she loved? She'd never know. The coat and its button were gone for ever.

Like Joe.

And Dad.

And the old city of Ypres which Rose had felt sleeping beneath the stones of the new town.

Perhaps none of it had happened at all.

And then, as she stood up, she saw her boots. They were lying discarded on the floor by the bed and they were caked in mud. Rose picked one up to look at it more closely. The mud was nasty yellowish stuff, thick and claggy, like clay. And it was still wet. It was the mud of the trenches, and it was as real as the sunlight on the wall and the carpet beneath her bare feet. She put the boot gently back down on the floor. She'd have to clean the mud off, she supposed. But not yet.

She wasn't quite ready to wash away the past.

Rose pulled up the blind. Sunshine flooded in, making the bright room even brighter. It was a beautiful day. The sort of blue winter's morning that reminded you of Christmas when you were little and you went for a walk in the park after breakfast with your mum and dad, riding your new scooter or clutching the giant cuddly animal that your grandad had bought you. Rose smiled as she remembered all those animals. One year it was a black panther with bright green eyes that scared her a bit. The next it was a huge orang-utan, bigger than she was, whose long ginger hairs got up her nose when she cuddled it. And then there was the year they'd stopped and drunk ginger beer (because it was Christmassy) in a chilly pub garden before going home to dinner. That was the last Christmas they'd had with Dad.

Outside, the not-square square sparkled in the morning sun. Rose watched a mother sweep her little boy up into her arms to give him a kiss, and a laughing teenage couple chase each other around the fountain before falling into each other's arms.

Of course. It was Valentine's Day.

Joe's day.

Rose remembered his face as he looked over his shoulder at her for the last time. She understood now why he'd done it, why he'd gone back to fight. It wasn't for his country, not really – it was like he said. He'd rather be dead than spend the rest of his life feeling bad about his mates.

But she still wished he hadn't, wished she could've convinced him to stay in England. What was it he said?

'People like us, Rose, we just want to live happy quiet lives, don't we? Little house. Enough to eat . . .'

That was all he'd wanted. And Rose wished with all her

heart he could have had it. But she knew now that you can't change the past. It doesn't mean you have to forget it, but you can't change it and you can't stay there. Perhaps, deep down, she'd always known it.

Rose turned away from the window and went to have a shower. She had the dirt of another century beneath her fingernails.

It was quite late by the time she arrived downstairs, glowing from her shower and glad to be out of her owl pyjamas and into some proper clothes. She didn't have another pair of shoes with her, so she'd cleaned her boots in the shower, washing the mud of the trenches away in a froth of strawberry-scented shower gel.

Everyone must have had their breakfast, because there was no one in the restaurant. Grandad had already gone out, Muriel explained, as she led Rose over to the table they'd sat at the night before where Rose had drunk hot chocolate and wondered what was going on. It was laid for breakfast now, with a plain white coffee cup, cereal bowl, plate . . .

And a heart wrapped in red foil.

Muriel smiled when she saw Rose's face. 'It's from your grandfather,' she said. 'He got up early this morning, asked me which of the chocolate shops would be open.'

Rose picked it up and smelled the chocolate through the foil. Grandad knew that Dad always gave her something on Valentine's Day. She thought of her mum; this was the first year she wouldn't get her roses from Dad, one for every year they'd been together. Rose was glad they were going home today.

'Where's Grandad now?' she said. 'Did he say?'

Muriel was finding it difficult to look her in the eye. 'I'm not quite sure,' she said, although she obviously was. 'He asked me to say he'd see you back here at midday,' she went on, trying to change the subject. 'I think you are catching your train this afternoon?'

'Yes,' said Rose. 'We'll be home by teatime.'

And she would buy some flowers for Mum at the station when they got to London, she thought. Not roses, no. Something cheerful and spring-like. She thought of the celandines she'd picked at the cemetery, and the ones Joe had been wearing in his buttonhole when they first met. Yes, she'd buy yellow flowers.

'But for now, breakfast!' Muriel seemed relieved that Rose wasn't asking any more questions about Grandad's whereabouts. 'Full English?'

Rose hadn't realised how hungry she was. After bacon, eggs, hot chocolate, three pieces of toast and the chocolate heart, she felt a lot better. She got up from the table, put on her parka and set off for a last walk around the city.

The streets glowed with life and happiness. Perhaps the ghost of the old city was finally laid to rest – Rose didn't feel her any more. The past was the past, she thought. It wanted to be remembered, but not relived. She'd spent too much time in the past, reliving her time with Dad, thinking about him, dreaming about him, sending him texts she knew he'd never read. Now she would just remember him and try to feel happy, not sad. And she'd help her mum do the same.

Rose found that her feet had taken her to the place where the road passed through the gap in the city ramparts. The great arch of the Menin Gate shone bone-white in the sunshine as she remembered her last promises to Joe: *Look after Tommy for me. And don't forget your present.* Rose smiled – a boy from the past had given her back her present. That wasn't what he'd meant, of course, but it was true.

Was this the place? The place they'd walked when they'd first met, where he'd told her he'd hidden the present? She tried to remember exactly what had happened on that cold February night a few hours and a hundred years ago. Joe had been on her right as they'd walked up this same street in the snow. She could almost feel the touch of his shoulder against hers.

Then Tommy – this was before he had his name – Tommy had rushed past them after the cat in a flurry of claws and snow. They'd had to get out of the way, she and Joe, and Tommy had chased the cat to the right of the road, where the ramparts went up.

There was grass there now, neatly tended, and a sign that told you all about the ceremony of the Last Post. And some bushes, growing close to the old wall.

Rose took a step nearer and dropped to her knees on the grass. She peered through the undergrowth. It was difficult to see . . .

But, but, but . . .

There was . . . there *was* a gap in the stones. She could see it, a dark hole in the wall, through the tangle of twigs.

It was still there. Their hiding place was still there.

Heart thudding, Rose pushed her way through the bushes and reached inside the hole. The twigs scratched her face, and a sharp stone was digging into one of her knees, but she didn't care.

'Good morning.' An amused voice with a slight accent.

It was the German boy, wearing a tartan fur-lined hat

with ear flaps, and pushing his bike as usual. Rose realised with a slight jolt of surprise that she was glad to see him.

'Hello,' she said, trying to look as if it was completely normal to be on your hands and knees in the middle of a bush on a chilly morning in Belgium. 'I'm just – looking for something,' she went on. 'Well, not looking, obviously, because I can't see anything. I'm more, sort of, feeling around for it. In this, um, hole.'

'I see.' He was the kind of person who never seemed surprised. 'Is it something you have lost?'

'No. Not really.' Rose decided to tell as much of the truth as would make sense. 'Someone left something here for me a long time ago. I promised to look for it.'

The boy seemed to accept this too. Rose was glad he didn't ask any more questions. She liked him for that.

'But I can't' – Rose was feeling around inside the hole again – 'I can't reach far enough. All I can feel is grit and stuff.'

'Can I help?' said the boy. 'My arms are perhaps a little longer?'

'OK.' Rose was grateful for the offer. 'Thanks.'

The boy parked his bike and crouched down beside her. She held the bushes out of the way while he put his arm inside the hole.

'It goes back quite a long way,' he said.

'Yes, but the boy – the *person* – who left the thing for me, he wasn't as tall as you, so . . .'

He continued to feel around, frowning with concentration. Rose watched his face.

'No?'

'No. I can't . . . just little stones and dead leaves and . . . oh . . . one moment.'

He shifted his weight so he was closer to the wall, then lay flat on his stomach so he could reach further into the hole, concentrating all his energy on his one-handed search. Rose continued to watch his face, her heart thumping so hard she thought he would hear it.

Please let it be there, whatever it is, please.

But the German boy's face didn't change. It still had the same look of frowning concentration.

'No. I'm sorry. It does not appear—'

He stopped. His face changed, the frown softening into a look of discovery.

He'd found something.

Rose couldn't speak. She kept her eyes on the boy's face as he brought his arm out. There was something in his hand, something dark with a string hanging from it. He looked at it briefly, then held it out to Rose.

'Is this it? The thing you expected?'

Rose took it. It was a heart, about the size of the palm of her hand, carved out of wood with a rotten leather thong threaded through a hole in the top.

And there was something written on it.

Rose brushed the dirt away and read the words that were carved into the surface of the heart:

'TO MY ROSE FROM YOUR VALENTINE'

Rose stared. She was unable to speak.

The German boy was looking over her shoulder. 'Is that your name?' His voice seemed to come from a very long way away. 'Rose?'

Rose nodded but she couldn't say anything. She was crying now, silent tears running down both cheeks, but she didn't try to wipe them away. It didn't seem to matter if anybody saw them.

She didn't know how they started to walk, she and the German boy. Neither of them suggested it. She just became aware that they had somehow ended up on the ramparts, following a winding path among the trees. Neither spoke. The boy didn't ask her why she was crying or try to make her stop. He just walked beside her, watching his feet on the path and glancing occasionally at her face as the tears continued to run down her chin and drip on to her parka.

Eventually they came to a bench overlooking the water that lay beyond the ramparts. It was set in long grass that was starred with celandines.

'Shall we . . .?' he said.

Rose nodded. She'd stopped crying now, so wiped her face with her sleeve and looked down at the dirty wooden heart clutched in her hand. She knew it was the best present she would ever have.

'It is a sad place,' said the boy, staring out over the water. 'This Ieper.'

He said the name of the city in the Flemish way. Rose waited for him to go on.

'We are all here because we lost someone,' he said. His words dropped into the silence like pebbles. 'My great-great-grandfather. He was killed at the end of the war, only one month before the Armistice.'

'Is that why you're here?' said Rose.

'In a way,' he replied. 'His sister, my great-great-aunt, came to visit his grave after the war. While she was here she met a Belgian boy, one that had survived, and she married him. So you see, I'm almost a native.'

'You've got Belgian cousins.'

'That's right.'

'The boys I saw you with last night?'

'Yes. They live on a farm outside the city. I visit them often for holidays. And you?'

'Me? I haven't got any Belgian cousins.'

The boy smiled. Even his smile was serious. 'You lost someone too?' he said. 'Is that why—?'

'My dad.' He looked so amazed that Rose almost laughed. 'Not in the war, obviously. Last year.'

'I see.'

He didn't say any of the things that people usually said, through embarrassment or pity, but just looked at her and waited. And then she told him something she'd never told anyone before, this boy from another country that she'd only just met.

'I still send him texts.'

'You do?' He didn't sound surprised. It was as if it was quite normal to send texts to a dead person.

'I did, anyway.'

The boy smiled his serious smile. 'Have you ever had a reply?'

Rose shook her head. She was smiling too now. 'Not so far.'

'Ach,' he said. 'Maybe one day.'

'I don't think I'll be sending them any more, actually.'

'No?'

Rose shook her head. 'It made me feel better for a bit,' she said. 'But now . . .'

The boy nodded as if he thought she'd made the right decision. 'You have got past that stage.'

Rose looked at him. He was right. 'Yes,' she said. 'I think I have.'

He got up. 'Shall we go back? Your grandfather may be wondering where you are.'

Rose had forgotten she was meant to meet Grandad at twelve. She checked her phone. 'Argh! It's ten to!'

'Then we must hurry.'

'Wait!'

He stopped, looking at her over his shoulder.

'I don't know your name,' said Rose.

He smiled. It was a gentle smile, not cheeky like Joe's, and it made Rose feel calm and happy.

'Did I not tell you?' he said. 'I'm sorry. It's Friedrich. But you can call me Fred.'

15

It was five past twelve by the time Rose and Fred got back to the hotel and Grandad was waiting outside with his bag all packed and ready to go. Rose rushed up.

'Grandad Grandad Grandad, sorry sorry sorry!'

'Not to worry, Cabbage, we've got enough time if you get a shift on.' Grandad accepted her kiss with a smile, his eyes resting on Fred. 'Hello again, young man.'

'You don't have to call him that, Grandad. He's got a name. It's Fred.'

'Pleased to meet you, Fred.' Grandad held out his hand and Fred shook it.

'You too, sir.'

'And thank you for the chocolate heart, Grandad. I've eaten it already.'

'That's all right. Every girl should have something on Valentine's Day. Isn't that right, Fred?'

Grandad winked and Fred smiled politely. Rose rolled

her eyes. It was the kind of thing that would've embarrassed her before. It didn't any more, she didn't know why.

'Actually, Rose,' Grandad continued. 'I've got another surprise for you.'

'What?'

'Stay there.'

Rose and Fred looked at each other as he went into the hotel, returning straight away with –

'*Tommy?!*'

The little dog pricked up his ears at the sound of his name. Grandad was holding him by a lead that was attached to a new red collar. Rose crouched down and scratched him in his favourite place behind the ears, enjoying the familiar feel of his wiry fur.

'Is that what you're going to call him?' said Grandad. 'Good name. Suits you, don't it, matey?'

There was something in the tone of his voice that made Rose look up. He sounded so terribly pleased with himself.

'What d'you mean? *Brian*?'

Grandad put on his look of comedy innocence. 'What d'you mean, what do I mean?'

'You said, is that what you're going to call him?'

'Did I? Oh, yeah. Well, he's got to have a name, hasn't he? If he's coming to live with you.'

'What?!'

'We've got it all arranged, haven't we, Muriel?'

Grandad's friend from the hotel had come out to join them. She nodded, smiling as she watched Rose's face shift between disbelief and delight.

'We have. I have asked all my neighbours about the dog and they agree that he is a *stray*.' She pronounced her newly discovered word with pride. 'No one owns him.

People feed him, but he needs a proper home.'

'So that's what you were up to this morning?' Rose could hardly believe it. She stood up. 'Oh, Grandad.' Then a thought struck her. 'What about Mum?'

'Panic ye not, Cabbage-face.' Grandad looked very smug. 'I rang her and she's agreed.'

'What? That we can take him home with us? Really?'

'Not straight away,' said Grandad. 'In a few weeks, after he's been through all the vet stuff – rabies injections, you know, all that. Muriel says she'll take care of it.'

'And then?'

'We'll jump back on the old Eurostar and pick him up!'

Rose couldn't speak. She dropped to her knees and buried her face in Tommy's fur. She was going to have a dog. And not just any dog. An amazing magical dog who existed outside of time and was the only creature in the whole world who knew what she'd been through. Who had helped her find Joe.

And she was going to be able to keep her last promise to her Valentine – and look after Tommy.

It was Fred who broke the silence. 'I could take care of him, if you prefer. Until you come and pick him up, of course.' He looked at Muriel. 'It may not be so convenient for you to have him in the hotel, I think? And my cousins live on a farm just outside the city. I know they will be pleased to help.'

Muriel shrugged and smiled. 'Well, it would certainly be better for the dog to stay on a farm—'

'Then it's settled!' Grandad sounded triumphant. 'If you're sure it will be all right with your family, Fred?'

'Of course,' he replied. 'They already have three dogs. One more will make no difference.' He turned to Rose, trying to hide the smile that was curling round his lips. 'And it will mean you have to come back and see me again.'

'Three weeks next Saturday?' said Grandad. 'That all right with you, Cabbage?'

Rose nearly laughed with happiness. 'What do *you* think, Grandad?'

Three weeks next Saturday would be trez, trez beans.

After that everything was a bit of a blur. Rose threw her clothes into her suitcase, Muriel called a taxi, and before Rose knew it she and Grandad were on their way to the station, bumping over the cobbles of Ypres for the last time.

Fred and Tommy had set off first (Fred left his bike locked up in the square) and they were waiting outside the station when the taxi arrived. Tommy was looking almost respectable in his brand-new collar. On the way, Fred had stopped at an engraving shop and bought Tommy a name tag in the shape of a bone, with Rose's phone number underneath Tommy's name.

Grandad shook Fred's hand, and Rose double-checked her number before burying her nose in Tommy's fur again.

'You're coming to London, Tommy,' she whispered. 'You're going to have to learn to speak English.'

Tommy grinned and wagged and looked at them all with his bright, interested eyes. Then, as Grandad started to limp his way across the car park to the station, Rose became aware that Fred was making awkward little coughing sounds. As she gave Tommy one last hug, he produced something from behind his back. It was a bunch of celandines.

'I—' He stopped and looked at his feet, before trying

again. 'They—'

Rose decided to help him out. She stood up. 'Are they for me?'

He nodded, still unable to look at her. 'Not as good as your other present,' he said. 'But . . .'

Rose looked down at the little yellow flowers then back up at Fred's serious grey eyes. 'They're lovely,' she said. 'Thank you.'

Before she could say any more there was a shout from Grandad: 'Rose!'

He was on the steps of the station, pointing at his watch. The train was about to arrive.

Rose turned to Fred. 'I'll see you in three weeks,' she said. 'Both of you,' she added, looking down at the dog.

'Wuff!' Tommy's polite little bark sounded different this time. He was going to London!

'ROSE!' Grandad called, more urgently this time.

Fred held out his hand. 'Goodbye, Rose.'

Rose smiled. He was such a serious boy. 'Bye,' she said.

Then, ignoring his hand, she stretched up, standing on tiptoe because he was so much taller than she was, and kissed him on the cheek. A handshake just seemed too formal after everything that had happened.

Her last sight of Ypres was of Fred standing on the station platform with Tommy beside him, one hand raised in farewell.

'What have you got there, Cabbage?'

They were ten minutes into the journey home. Rose was looking at her wooden heart while Grandad munched a custard cream, showering crumbs all over the table. Rose discreetly removed one from the back of her hand.

'Someone gave it to me.' She passed it across the table to him.

'What a nice thing. Looks quite old.' Grandad put on his glasses to examine it more closely. '"To my Rose",' he read aloud. '"From your Valentine".' He peered at Rose over his glasses, his face full of questions. '"To my Rose"?' he repeated. 'Is that you, Cabbage?'

Rose nodded.

Grandad looked down at the heart and traced the letter R with his forefinger. 'But—' He stopped. and looked at Rose again. 'But this thing – it's *old*. Isn't it? How can it be—?'

Rose didn't know what to say. She wasn't going to lie to her grandad, make up some story about the person who gave it to her finding it or buying it in a second-hand shop or something. But she couldn't explain to him what had really happened, how she'd really come to own the heart. How could she? She didn't understand it herself.

'Bit tricky to explain,' she said, hoping he wouldn't ask her anything else.

Grandad shrugged and handed the heart back. 'You young girls with your secrets. I don't know. Have a biscuit.'

'No thanks, Brian, you're all right.'

Grandad smiled. 'Going to that party of yours tonight?' he said. 'We should be back in time.'

Rose had forgotten about Grace's party. It didn't seem like such a bad idea now. 'Yes,' she said, as if the idea had only just occurred to her. 'Yes, I think I might.'

She watched the fields as they slipped past the window, wreathed in the mists of the February afternoon. The perfectly round ponds didn't make her feel sick any more.

It just seemed nice that something pretty had come out of something so horrible. And the neat manicured cemeteries with their rows of white graves didn't fill her with fear and sadness. They reminded her of Joe.

Rose looked at the precious wooden heart on the table in front of her, next to the little bunch of celandines, and thought of Joe's grin and Dad's eyes and the feel of Tommy's fur beneath her fingers and everything that had happened in that one little city with three names.

She understood now why it wanted to be Ieper. It had moved on. The past was important, but so was the future. And the present.

She would remember to buy those yellow flowers for Mum when they got to London. The biggest bunch she could afford.

Her thoughts were interrupted by a buzz from her phone. She looked at the screen, aware that Grandad was watching her face.

It was from *Mummob*:

Hello love, you ok? Can't wait to see you tonight

Then, three kisses:

x x x

Rose suddenly wanted to see her mum very much. She wouldn't be able to tell her what had happened, about Joe and everything. But she'd give her the flowers, and they'd hug and Rose would hide her face in Mum's hair and breathe in her smell of baby lotion and shampoo and coffee. Just like she used to before Dad died.

I'm fine, she replied. *Can't wait to see you too*

And she sent three kisses back:

x x x

AFTERWORD

How *Valentine Joe* Began

I grew up surrounded by stories about the First World War. My dad's mum was a nurse, his dad a soldier who'd been one of her patients. My mum's father was a pilot and her mum, who was fourteen when the war broke out, told me about watching the newly recruited soldiers marching down the high street of the London suburb where she grew up, through the cheering, flag-waving crowds and past the shops selling toys and vegetables and ladies' hats. One young soldier had a rose in his buttonhole which he threw to her. My gran never knew what happened to him, of course, but she kept that rose until it fell apart many years later. She also remembered going into the kitchen at home and finding the housekeeper crying over the sink. Her son was away fighting in France and she was washing his long all-in-one underwear which had been sent back to her in a bag of laundry. It was caked in mud right up to the armpits.

I always thought the strangest, saddest thing about that story was that these young men were fighting in the most terrible war the world has ever seen, miles away from home in a foreign country and in unimaginably horrible conditions – *but they sent their washing home to their mothers . . .*

Although these stories made the war feel very real to me (frighteningly real in some ways – for years I had a recurring nightmare that I was a soldier in the trenches), they were all second-hand. They belonged to other people. I never heard the voices of the people who had actually been there.

Until a few years ago.

When my uncle died, I was given a tatty old cardboard folder that had been hidden away in his house for years. Inside there were hundreds of sheets of thin yellowish paper that smelled of dust and mildew and were closely covered with blobby writing in the purple-black ink that was used in typewriters a hundred years ago.

They were letters, written by my grandfather to his parents during the First World War.

His name was Fred, but my sister and I called him Fuffy. Like Rose, my older sister had overheard our gran calling her husband by his first name and tried to copy her. Because she wasn't big enough to pronounce it properly, 'Freddie' became 'Fuffy'. And he stayed that way for us until he died when I was seven.

Although I was quite little when he died, I remember him very well. He was the sort of man who made you feel like you were the most interesting, amazing and clever person he'd ever met and that you and he were going to have the most incredible adventures together. I always knew he'd been involved in the First World War, first as an underage soldier and then as a pilot in the Royal Flying Corps, which later became the RAF.

But I didn't know about those letters.

When war was declared in August 1914, the rule was that you had to be eighteen to join the army, nineteen to be sent abroad where the fighting was going on. But, like many boys in their teens, Fred must have been caught up in the feeling of patriotism that swept the country. Perhaps he thought the war would be exciting, even fun. He almost certainly didn't think he might be killed.

So he lied about his age and joined up. He was sixteen.

He wasn't the only one. In the early years of the war, the

need for recruits was so high that it's thought recruiting officers often turned a blind eye or even encouraged boys to lie about their age. Fred joined the Seaforth Highlanders and, along with his best friend Fraser, travelled from his home in South London to train in the Scottish Highlands with his regiment. From there, he wrote his funny, cheerful letters home several times a week, describing the food, his fellow soldiers and his excitement at being issued with a kilt as part of his uniform. Now, when I re-read those letters, I try and imagine the smiling fluffy-haired old man in the yellow jumper who I remember, as the cheeky 'Cockney' (which was what the Scottish recruits called him) who wrote them.

I'm very glad Fred did write those letters and that some-one (I like to think it was his poor, worried mum) typed them out and preserved them so carefully. Because Fred's letters are the reason I became interested in the boy soldiers of the First World War and found out about Valentine Joe.

Valentine Joe Strudwick was a real person. He was born on Valentine's Day 1900, in Dorking, Surrey. His dad was a gardener and his mum earned money by doing people's washing. Joe left school at thirteen and worked for his uncle who was a local coal merchant. And then, in August 1914, everything changed. War was declared with Germany and, just like my grandfather, Joe joined up.

The date was January 1915 and he was fourteen.

My grandfather was lucky. Before his regiment was sent overseas to fight, he caught pneumonia from marching around in the snow wearing his much-loved kilt. An army doctor realised he was underage and sent him home to London.

Joe wasn't lucky.

After a few weeks' training he was sent to Belgium where his two best friends were killed and he was gassed. After recovering in hospital in England, he went back to the Front and on 14 January 1916, exactly one month before his sixteenth birthday, he was killed.

Joe is buried at Essex Farm Cemetery, near Ieper, where you can go and put celandines on his grave.

Rebecca Stevens
Brighton, 2014